Where pow ns

Welcome to a rich and verdant land—where rugged, sexy men and bold, strong women flourish. One powerful family has been living and loving here for generations. Watch as twelve passionate tales of old fortunes and new futures thrill this close community…

Everybody's Talking
Barbara Kaye

When Lori Porter discovers there's money missing from an account she handles, she asks Cody Hendricks for help. But when Lori and Cody team up, she finds his motives are more than strictly business!

Don't miss this the exciting conclusion to Silhouette's twelve-book series! Every book reverberates with the rhythm of this wild land, and we hope you'll all be coming back soon!

About the author:

Barbara Kaye is a family woman with five grown children, who lives in Oklahoma and is able to offer her readers an insightful look at human nature.

Everybody's Talking

BARBARA KAYE

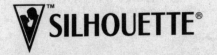

DID YOU PURCHASE THIS BOOK WITHOUT A COVER?
If you did, you should be aware it is **stolen property** as it was
reported *unsold and destroyed* by a retailer. Neither the author nor
the publisher has received any payment for this book.

*All the characters in this book have no existence outside the imagination of
the author, and have no relation whatsoever to anyone bearing the same
name or names. They are not even distantly inspired by any individual
known or unknown to the author, and all the incidents are pure invention.*

*All Rights Reserved including the right of reproduction in whole or in part
in any form. This edition is published by arrangement with Harlequin
Enterprises II B.V. The text of this publication or any part thereof may not
be reproduced or transmitted in any form or by any means, electronic or
mechanical, including photocopying, recording, storage in an
information retrieval system, or otherwise, without the written
permission of the publisher.*

*This book is sold subject to the condition that it shall not, by way of trade
or otherwise, be lent, resold, hired out or otherwise circulated without the
prior consent of the publisher in any form of binding or cover other than
that in which it is published and without a similar condition including this
condition being imposed on the subsequent purchaser.*

*Silhouette and Colophon are registered trademarks of
Harlequin Books S.A., used under licence.*

*First published in Great Britain 2000
Silhouette Books, Eton House, 18-24 Paradise Road,
Richmond, Surrey TW9 1SR*

© Harlequin Enterprises II B.V. 1993

Special thanks and acknowledgement to Barbara Kaye for her
contribution to the River Deep series.

Special thanks and acknowledgement to Sutton Press Inc. for its
contribution to the concept for the River Deep series.
This series was originally called Crystal Creek

ISBN 0 373 82524 2

113-0101

*Printed and bound in Spain
by Litografia Rosés S.A., Barcelona*

River Deep™

A Note from the Author

The town of Crystal Creek, Texas, is not all cattle
barons, cowboys, oilmen, beauty queens and
performers. The majority of its citizens lead quiet,
ordinary lives—hardly the stuff of novels. In
Everybody's Talking, accountant Lori Porter and
banker Cody Hendricks seems to be just such
people. Lori, especially, feels her life is in a rut.
Then she and Cody become involved in a case of
embezzlement, and life no longer is ordinary.
However, the most extraordinary thing about it is
their sudden attraction to each other. I hope Lori
and Cody become two of your favourite River Deep
characters.

Barbara Kaye

PROLOGUE

HANK TRAVIS SLUMPED in a chair near the fireplace. His old bones felt cold most of the time, but simply watching the licking flames seemed to warm him some. There had been a time when he would have been outside in his shirtsleeves in this kind of weather, but sadly those days were gone forever. A couple of decades ago when he was in his seventies…

His thoughts halted. It often pained him to realize that his years on earth were approaching the century mark, but then he would remind himself that being so old wasn't too bad when he considered the alternative. He sure couldn't complain. He'd lived a long life blessedly free of ailments, and it was his rock-solid belief that he had lived during the absolute best time in the history of civilization. The things he had seen, the changes that had come along!

He doubted his grandson or great-grandchildren could imagine the wonder a young man felt when he saw his first telephone or his first automobile. Hank could remember when the sound of an airplane brought people scurrying outdoors to stare up at the sky, awestruck. Would there ever again be another time like the twentieth century?

He squinted through his wire-rimmed glasses at his grandson, J.T. McKinney, and J.T.'s wife, Cynthia. They were seated on the sofa across the room, holding hands like a couple of lovebirds. Cynthia, now in the final month of her pregnancy, looked prettier than ever to Hank's notion. She'd lost some of that cool, gaunt Boston blueblood air and looked…well, matronly and sweet.

His gaze shifted to J.T. Hank thought his grandson looked pretty hale and hearty, not at all like a man who had suffered a heart attack during the past year. The old man had often wondered if the attack had been prompted by cavorting with a pretty wife twenty years younger than he was. *Course, when I was fifty-six, I was pretty frisky with the ladies, and it never hurt me none. What about that little gal in Ozona who'd had the hots for me when I was almost sixty?*

The fire had warmed him and made him drowsy. A curious feeling of well-being came over him. Hank's eyes drooped, and his chin fell forward on his chest. Within seconds, he had slid into sleep.

Across the room, Cynthia McKinney watched him with concern. It seemed to her that Hank was slipping badly, though no one ever talked about it. J.T. didn't. Tyler, Cal and Lynn, J.T.'s adult children, didn't. Neither did Virginia Parks, the housekeeper, nor Lettie Mae Reese, the cook. But Cynthia was certain they all had noticed the gauntness, the increased grumpiness that came across as a sort of bravado, and these frequent catnaps. She sighed inaudibly. She was beginning to relax about J.T.'s health. All outward signs pointed to a complete recovery, and Dr. Purdy had assured her over and over that such was the case. But Hank wasn't going to recover; he would only get worse.

How strange that she had become rather fond of the old goat. A year ago she wouldn't have thought it possible. Cynthia smiled secretively. Oh, what a time he had given her! Hank had hated his grandson's choice for a wife. She was too young, too snooty, too *Boston* to suit him, and he hadn't made any bones about it, either.

Now she liked to think his attitude toward her had changed, that maybe he even liked her, but she was certain she would never hear such an admission from the lips of Hank Travis.

Suddenly Hank's eyes flew open. He shook his head as if trying to clear it, then looked around, seemingly disoriented. Beside Cynthia, J.T. straightened, his attention arrested.

"Something wrong, Grandpa?" he asked.

Hank frowned and said nothing for a few seconds. Then he asked, "When was the last time you talked to Carolyn?"

J.T. and Cynthia exchanged puzzled glances. Carolyn was J.T.'s late wife's sister. She owned the Circle T, the ranch adjoining J.T.'s Double C, and she had remained a much-loved member of the family. "Oh, I don't know," J.T. said. "I usually talk to her a couple of times a week at least. Why?"

Hank scratched the stubble on his chin. "I must'a dozed off for a minute 'cause I had a dream. Somethin's about to happen to her."

Cynthia stiffened. Hank's dreams or visions or whatever they could be called were legendary in the McKinney clan. When she had first come to the Double C, she had laughed at them, unable to believe anyone actually put any faith in such nonsense. But she no longer laughed because Hank had just been right too often. Now, Cynthia was willing to accept that Hank really did "see" things no one else did. "Is she in some kind of danger?" she asked fearfully.

"Nope. It's more like somebody's got a hand in

her till, is stealin' from her. You ought'a tell her
to keep her eyes open.''

"But Lori takes care of Carolyn's money,
Grandpa,'' J.T. said. "Lori would never let anything happen to a dime of it.''

"I'm jus' tellin' you what I saw, goddammit!''
Hank barked. "Somebody's stealin' from her, and
I think you ought'a tell her.''

Cynthia pondered that and glanced at her watch.
It was after nine o'clock on Sunday night, and Carolyn was an early-to-bed type. Was it too late to
call?

No, she decided, not for something this important. Maybe she was being foolish, but if Hank felt
it was important, it probably was. She struggled to
her feet. "I think I'm going to do just that right
now.''

J.T. put a restraining hand on her arm. "Sit
down, hon. I'll call her in the morning. You should
stay off your feet.''

"Dr. Purdy says I can do anything I feel like
doing, and right now I feel like calling Carolyn,''
Cynthia said as she headed for the telephone in
J.T.'s office.

CHAPTER ONE

MONDAY MORNING dawned crisp and clear in the Hill Country of Central Texas. Lori Porter, out for her customary morning stroll, scanned the sky as dawn pinkened its rim. A red-tailed hawk soared above the cedar-covered limestone hills, searching for prey. Lori envied the bird its freedom and wished she, too, could have a hawk's-eye view of her surroundings, for they were beautiful, even as winter approached. And in the midst of the rustic loveliness stood the Circle T Ranch, Lori's home for the past few years.

As her morning walk ended, the ranch began to stir for the day. Hired hands came out of the bunkhouse; those who lived in the nearby town of Crystal Creek drove through the front gate. All of them invariably drove pickups, which they parked behind the bunkhouse. Lori spotted Karl Walters, the ranch foreman, heading for the corral. As usual, he'd been up and about before anyone else. He saw her and waved; she waved back.

Several lights were on in the main house where Lori's cousin Carolyn lived with her new husband, Vernon Trent. Quickening her step, Lori hurried past her own quarters and entered the house through the back door.

Vernon was seated at the long oak table that occupied the center of the homey kitchen. He looked up from the newspaper when the door opened. "Good morning, Lori."

"Good morning, Vern. Mmm, that coffee smells good."

The tall, slender, blond woman at the stove turned with a smile. "Good morning, Lori," Carolyn said.

"Good morning, Caro." Lori poured a cup of coffee and carried it to the table.

"Your cousin has some news for you," Vernon informed her.

"Oh?" Lori turned to Carolyn with curiosity.

"Cynthia called last night. Seems Hank had a dream about me. He says someone's got a hand in my till."

Lori frowned. "How could that be? *I* take care of your money, and I can account for every dime of it."

"I know. That was the first thing Vern mentioned when I told him about the call," Carolyn said. "I guess Hank can't be right one-hundred percent of the time, but—"

"He usually is," Lori finished for her.

"I know."

"So," Vernon said, "Caro and I have about decided it's not money someone's taking. Maybe it's property."

"Like gear, saddles, something like that," Carolyn explained.

"Or cattle?" Lori suggested.

Carolyn's eyes widened. "But I know everyone on this ranch. I can't believe any of them would steal *cattle* from me."

"Remember the incident at the Double C last year?" Lori reminded her. "J.T. knew Chase Bennett, too, but that didn't stop Chase from stealing his cows."

Carolyn and Vernon exchanged anxious glances. "You ought to look into it, Caro," he said.

Carolyn nodded. "I'll have Karl take inventory. I haven't missed anything, but the theft might have been recent."

The timer on the oven buzzed. Bending, Carolyn pulled out a pan of muffins, put them in a napkin-lined basket and carried them to the table. "How's Marian?" she asked, referring to Lori's mother, her own aunt.

"Fine as far as I know. Looking forward to the Christmas holidays, I'm sure, even though her holidays never seem very restful to me. She spends them getting ready for midterm exams and making out next semester's lessons."

"She's sure been teaching a long time," Carolyn remarked. "A very industrious lady. It's hard to believe she and my ne'er-do-well father had the same set of parents. How's Anna?" she then asked, mentioning Lori's paternal grandmother, who lived with Marian.

Lori rolled her eyes. "Grandma's fine. She never changes. The saddest part of her life was my divorce, and down deep inside her Italian heart she honestly believes Michael and I are going to patch things up one of these days."

Carolyn grinned. "After five years?"

At that moment the kitchen door opened and Beverly, Carolyn's daughter, put in an appearance. Dressed in a fluffy blue robe, without makeup and with her fantastic blond hair disheveled, she still was the picture of loveliness. "Morning, everybody," she said and made for the coffeepot. Pouring a cup, she joined the group at the table.

"Is Jeff still in town?" Carolyn asked idly.

Beverly's eyes clouded. "No. When does he ever stay parked more than a couple of days?

Sometimes I wish Grandpa Hank had never mentioned that property of his.''

"That's pretty selfish, dear,'' Carolyn admonished. ''Jeff had been looking for a drilling site for months when he hooked up with Hank.''

"I know, but I sure didn't expect him to have to spend so much time there.''

"Why don't you go with him?'' Lori asked.

"Because sitting around a drilling site all day is *so-o-o* boring.''

Just then Vernon uttered a sound of disgust and slammed the newspaper down on the table. ''The damned silly ways the government finds to spend our money!'' He drained his coffee and reached for another muffin, standing as he did. ''Gotta run, ladies. There's a young couple coming up from San Antonio to look for a weekend retreat. See you tonight, darling.'' He bent to give Carolyn a kiss, a lingering one, Lori noticed. ''Bye, Lori.''

"Goodbye, Vern. I hope they buy something.''

"Lord, so do I. The market's been flatter than a pancake lately, and this is never a good time of year in the real estate business. Bye, Bev. See you later.'' He gave Carolyn's shoulder an affectionate pat and left the room.

Lori loved watching Carolyn and Vernon together even though their obvious love for each other tugged at her heart in ways that weren't altogether pleasant. It reminded her of the sterility of her own love life. In the years since her divorce from Michael Porter, she had been involved with only one man, Lou Chaney, the assistant football coach at Crystal Creek High. He'd left in August to take a position with a high school in Austin. For a time they had continued to see each other occasionally. Either she would go to Austin or he would come to Crystal Creek, but the relationship had gradually died without too much regret on Lori's part. Looking back, she saw that she and Lou had been keeping each other company more than anything. Certainly it had not been an exciting romance.

And that, Lori thought ruefully, pretty well summed up her entire existence. It was orderly and pleasant, but never, ever exciting.

"Are you going to the bank as usual this morning?" Carolyn asked, snapping Lori out of her musing.

"Yes."

"I'd like to go with you. I've been thinking about that savings account Frank opened just before he died. I think I'll close it out and put the money in one of the jumbo accounts. It'll earn more interest that way, right?"

"Right. I told you that last summer."

"I know, but I forgot. And I have some other errands I want to run. We'll just make a morning of it, okay?"

"Sounds good to me. Oh, Caro, these muffins are out of this world!"

"It's a new recipe, just loaded with things that are good for you."

"It's hard to believe something that tastes this good is good for you." Lori polished off the muffin and her coffee, then stood and carried her dishes to the sink to rinse them and put them in the dishwasher. "We'll leave about nine-thirty, if that's all right."

"That's fine," Carolyn said. "But first, I've got to go find Karl. If Hank says someone's stealing from me, someone probably is stealing from me."

"Want to come into town with us, Bev?" Lori asked.

"Oh...I don't guess so, thanks just the same. I think Lynn's sort of at loose ends today, too. I'll go over to the Double C and watch her rub down horses or something."

Smiling, Lori left the house, skirted the swimming pool and walked to a small building located some distance away. It had once been a garage, then a storage area for ranch wagons and the like.

When she had arrived at the Circle T, it had been abandoned, and Lori had seen its possibilities even then. But she'd never done anything about it. She had simply moved into the main house with Carolyn and Beverly. The arrangement had worked fine as long as there were only the three women, but from time to time Lori had eyed the little structure out back, thinking what a nice place it could be with a little attention.

Carolyn's marriage to Vernon had finally galvanized her into action. The newlyweds, she'd decided, needed their privacy. Now she had transformed the old garage into a lovely two-room studio, decorated in the bright colors she loved. Its interior still had a brand-new smell, for she had lived in it only a few weeks. Opening the door, she all but caressed the house with her eyes.

Lori often wondered what path her life might have taken if Carolyn hadn't insisted she come to the Circle T after the divorce. "Just for a little while," her cousin had said. "It's peaceful here, a good place to get yourself back on track." Now the little while had stretched into years. Carolyn didn't want her to leave, and Lori had come to think of the ranch as home.

Everything had turned out far better than she could have hoped. Since she was an accountant, she had offered to keep the ranch's books and do Carolyn's taxes in return for room and board. But as soon as it had become apparent that that alone wouldn't keep her busy enough, she had let it be known around that her services were available to other ranchers. She now had a long list of clients and was at last financially independent. Michael had said she'd never make it without him, but she had, and it felt good.

Life had settled into a comfortable routine. Or rut, Lori amended. Predictable and uneventful, at least for her. How she longed for something or someone to come along and shake things up a bit. A man would be the obvious solution, but given her conservative, reserved nature, Lori admitted she seemed to attract the solid, prosaic types like Lou, who lived and breathed football. To Lou, nothing on earth was more exciting than being on the ten-yard line with a minute to play.

As Lori crossed the living room to go into the bathroom for a shower, the phone on the desk in her bedroom rang. Reversing direction, she went to answer it.

"Lori Porter," she said crisply.

"Is that any way for a woman to answer the phone?" an admonishing voice on the other end of the line asked.

"Grandma!" Lori cried brightly, then immediately sobered. "Is anything wrong?"

"No, nothing's wrong, but I have a piece of news for you. Francis is getting married."

"Uncle Francis?" Lori exclaimed. "Who in the heck is he marrying?"

"Her name is Henrietta. She's from Houston. Francis proposed after knowing her only a few weeks."

The news was so startling Lori had to laugh. Francis, Anna's youngest son, was unquestionably the most colorless character Lori had ever known. Like the infamous man who came to dinner, he had shown up to visit the San Antonio branch of the DeMarco clan some fifteen years ago and was still there. He was fifty and had never been married. Lori tried without success to envision the type of woman who would want to marry Francis after having known him only a few weeks.

"What's she like?"

A pause followed. Then, "She has all this red hair—I'm sure she dyes it—and an enormous bosom that jiggles when she laughs. She's...well, you'll just have to meet her yourself."

It wasn't so much what Anna said as the way she said it that informed Lori her grandmother disapproved of the match. And Anna DeMarco disapproved of things the way she did everything else—unreservedly. Lori felt rather sorry for the unknown Henrietta. "I can hardly wait."

"So, Lori darling, if Francis can get married, surely you can, too. Have you met anyone yet?"

Ah, Lori thought. *So that's what's on her mind.* It was odd that Lou had never really counted with Anna. He was, according to her grandmother, in a line of work not known for its job security nor its ability to generate scads of income. When it came to a husband for Lori, Anna dreamed of a CEO or a pediatrician or, at the very least, a college president. "No, Grandma, I haven't met anybody. If and when I do, I promise you'll be the first to hear about it."

"Who are you going to meet on a ranch? Cowboys! Darling, you're forty years old!"

"And not getting any younger, right?"

Lori heard a sigh of exasperation. "Never mind," Anna said. "It's impossible to talk to you about this. Now then, do you have any idea how long it's been since you've come to see your mother and myself?"

Lori experienced a pang of guilt, not an unusual reaction when she was speaking to her grandmother. "I'm sorry, but this is such a busy time of year for me and…"

"If you were married, you wouldn't have to work."

"That's not necessarily true. I know plenty of married women who work."

"All your mother and I want is for you to meet a nice boy and settle down."

"What would a nice boy want with a forty-year-old woman?"

Anna sighed again. "You'll be here for Thanksgiving, won't you?"

"Of course. I wouldn't miss it."

"Then I'm writing it down on my calendar. There! It's done."

Lori smiled. When her grandmother wrote something on her calendar, it was as though it had been etched in stone. Suddenly she caught a glimpse of the clock on her desk. "Grandma, I'm awfully sorry, but I've got to run. I have to go to the bank and Carolyn wants to go with me. I haven't even showered yet, and I hate to keep her waiting."

"Oh, of course, of course. Then we'll definitely see you a week from Thursday?"

"Definitely."

"And, Lori darling, if you should meet someone between now and then, please feel free to bring him along."

"All right, Grandma, but don't count on an extra plate, okay?"

"All right. You take care of yourself."

"You, too. Bye, I love you."

"I love you, too, darling. Goodbye."

Hanging up, Lori sprinted for the bathroom, smiling and shaking her head. Sometimes it seemed as though her divorce had been more traumatic for Anna than it had been for her.

Little did her grandmother know that she didn't regret the absence of a man in Lori's life nearly as much as Lori herself did.

CHAPTER TWO

At PRECISELY EIGHT-THIRTY, half an hour before the glass doors of Southwest Bank would swing open to the public, Cody Hendricks, the branch manager, climbed the steps of the building and reached in his pocket for his key. Before using it, he checked for the all-clear signal—a small green card placed inconspicuously at the bottom of the glass panel next to the door, put there by the security man who was first in the building every morning. Had it not been there, Cody would have alerted the police that something was amiss inside the bank. However, it was where it should be. He turned the key and entered the building.

The Crystal Creek branch of Southwest Bank was a modern steel-and-glass structure that loomed large over the stately Victorian courthouse across the street in the town square. The bank was easily the community's most impressive commercial building. Its lobby was spacious and beautifully appointed. Behind Cody, the bank employees began filing through the door and taking their positions. He turned and went down a carpeted stairway to the vault in the basement.

There, two men were waiting—the security officer and the duty officer. The three men chatted for a few minutes, then fell silent as eight-forty neared. When they heard the faint click behind the massive steel door signaling that the overnight time lock had switched off, the security officer entered a combination, the duty officer another; then the two of them swung open the door. Having supervised the routine opening of the vault, Cody returned to the main lobby and climbed the stairs to his office on the mezzanine.

He spent some time reviewing loan applications. Then he fielded half a dozen phone calls, all involving civic matters. That done, he left his office to stand at the balcony overlooking the main lobby and watch the activity below with an air of proprietary pride. As usual on a Monday morning, the bank was busy. Satisfaction radiated from his eyes as a steady stream of customers poured in and out of the building. It was incredible really how much he had come to like the place.

But then, he had imagined he would. To the utter confusion of his family, he had all but begged to be assigned to the Crystal Creek branch when its former manager retired. "It's a chance to run an entire bank, not just one department," he'd explained, but no one, least of all his father, had understood. "You'll die of boredom," had been the prediction, but at the time Cody had been desperate for something. He'd thought a change, the more drastic the better, was in order.

There had been even more to it than simply wanting a change. At the time he had been going through the not-unusual angst of a man in his early forties—studying his physique in the mirror, looking for gray hairs and wrinkles, no longer thinking how many years lay ahead but wondering how many were left. It had been a difficult time.

But coming to Crystal Creek had solved that. By comparison with the flagship branch in Houston, the Crystal Creek bank was tiny indeed, but here he set policy. Here, when people wanted to see the "big man," they wanted to see him. This bank was his. Above all, here he felt unfettered by the rules and restrictions that had ordered and measured his life since the cradle.

And he was making the most of it. He had become a solid citizen and a community leader. Already the Crystal Creek branch's roster of depositors had grown to almost twice that of First National, their closest competitor, a fact not lost on the big shots in Houston. Cody smiled as his eyes once again swept the busy lobby. He would have liked to go down and personally shake every customer's hand. At that moment, a slender, shapely woman in a green dress walked through the entrance, and his smile grew broader. The cool, reserved Mrs. Porter. Lori had the face of a dark-haired angel, the body of a goddess and the agreeable but reserved manner he associated with royalty. There was something about her that intrigued him in an unusually vigorous way. Maybe it was her aloofness. It made a man long to get inside her head and find out what made her tick.

Last summer, when he was new in Crystal Creek, he had attended some sort of social affair at the country club. Lori had been there on the arm of a brawny fellow named Lou Chaney, one of the coaches at the local high school. By doing nothing more extraordinary than walking into the ballroom, Lori had become the focal point of Cody's attention. A few discreet inquiries had furnished the information that she and the coach were an ''item.'' Cody still remembered the regret he'd felt.

A few months later, he'd read in the local weekly that Coach Chaney had accepted a position at an Austin high school, and he'd vaguely wondered if Lori was now unattached. Not long after that, however, he'd spotted them having dinner at the Longhorn Coffee Shop, so he'd supposed they still were together. Chaney was pretty smart. Lori would be worth a forty-mile trip any day of the week.

This morning, right on Lori's heels was her cousin, Carolyn Townsend. No, it wasn't Townsend anymore, was it? She had recently married Vernon Trent. Carolyn's Circle T Ranch was one of the bank's more valued accounts. Though Lori came to the bank without fail every Monday morning, it was unusual to see Carolyn with her. Cody watched the two women with more than average interest. Carolyn obviously was heading for Helen Merriwether, the head cashier, while Lori marched straight to Mary Alice Priest's cage. He'd noticed that Lori always used the same teller, even if it meant waiting. The fact he'd ever paid any attention to that highlighted his unusual powers of observation when it came to her.

As if drawn by a magnet, Cody's gaze settled on her. She was waiting for Mary Alice to complete the transaction with the man ahead of her. Then the man left, and Lori stepped forward. She and Mary Alice always greeted each other like long-lost relatives, leading Cody to wonder if perhaps they were in some way related. It seemed to him that half of Crystal Creek's citizens were related to the other half.

Smiling, he turned on his heels. Satisfied that all was well with Southwest Bank this Monday morning, he went back into his office. It was time to get to work.

"THERE YOU GO, Lori," Mary Alice said, shoving a deposit slip toward her.

"Thanks." Lori took the slip and placed it inside her checkbook. "I guess while I'm here I'd better get some cash." As she wrote her check, she asked, "How's Norma?"

"Oh, some days Mama feels pretty good, other days not so good."

"The last time I went to the shop for a haircut, I really needed a manicure, too, but Norma wasn't there."

Mary Alice nodded ruefully. "I know. She has to miss work sometimes. Her back really gives her a fit, you know. I've begged her to see a specialist in Austin or San Antonio, but she says she can't afford it, that Dr. Purdy does what anyone else would do and doesn't charge half so much."

"That's a shame. Back trouble must be a terrible thing to have to live with." Lori finished writing her check and shoved it toward the teller. "By the way, I want to thank you for suggesting me to Sam Peterson. He's now my newest client.''

"Don't mention it," Mary Alice said as she counted out some bills. "I'm always happy to do something for a friend."

Lori was pleased that the young teller considered her a friend. Their friendship had begun some two years ago when Lori had come into the bank one Monday morning to find Mary Alice agitated and practically in tears over a letter she had received from Internal Revenue. It had been a form letter informing her that she had failed to report certain income and owed IRS more taxes plus a penalty. Mary Alice, it turned out, had cashed some savings bonds and forgotten about them. Lori was able to straighten it out in no time, something anyone familiar with tax laws could have done. But in Mary Alice's eyes, Lori had virtually saved her from debtor's prison, and her gratitude had not waned one iota.

Usually the two women saw each other only when Lori came to the bank, but on a few occasions they'd had lunch together. Mary Alice had a quality that tugged at Lori's heart in some unfathomable way. She was such a solitary individual, painfully shy and retiring. She wasn't pretty in the accepted sense of the word, but she was attractive with her long ash-blond hair and slender, boyish figure. Now in her mid-twenties, she still lived with her mother. If she had a boyfriend or even a close girlfriend, she'd never mentioned it to Lori.

But the quality that stood out most was Mary Alice's childlike eagerness for acceptance. One got the impression she would do anything to be liked, which meant she probably could be easily taken advantage of. And that was a pity. Lori liked the young teller; she really did.

Lori scooped up the bills Mary Alice pushed toward her and put them in her wallet. "Well, I'll see you next week, Mary Alice. Please give Norma my regards and tell her I'm very sorry about her back."

"I'll do that. Thanks, Lori."

Lori walked away, scanning the lobby for Carolyn. Spotting her, she moved in the direction of the head cashier's desk, but she had taken only a few steps when she noticed the angry expression on her cousin's face. Carolyn obviously was in some kind of argument with Helen Merriwether, who was an old friend. What on earth could those two be arguing about?

Puzzled, Lori looked at the cashier. Helen was a likable widow in her fifties who had been working at the bank "forever." She was always friendly but briskly professional. Right now, however, she looked upset and flustered.

Lori hurried to her cousin's side. "Is something wrong, Caro?"

"Indeed there is!" Carolyn snapped. "It seems the bank's records show there are two thousand dollars less in this account than my records show."

"I'm certain we can get to the bottom of this," Helen said nervously.

Eyes blazing, Carolyn looked up at Lori. "They say I withdrew the two thousand in October. I haven't lost my mind, have I? Did we withdraw money from the account in October?"

Lori took a seat beside Carolyn and shook her head. "No, I'm sure we didn't. I would remember. That account hasn't been touched since the day Frank opened it."

Carolyn turned to Helen. "There has been some kind of dreadful mistake, and it wasn't ours. Now I want this straightened out immediately, Helen. I'm very unhappy about it."

"I don't blame you." Helen's voice quivered as she picked up the phone and punched a button. Lori noticed the cashier was trembling. "Please let me speak to Mr. Hendricks, Martha. It's very important." A few seconds passed, then she said, "Mr. Hendricks, this is Helen. Can you come down here? There seems to be a problem. Yes, thank you.'' Replacing the receiver, she folded her hands on the desk. ''The manager will be down in a minute, Carolyn. I'm sure he'll have this straightened out in no time.''

''He'd better.'' Carolyn sniffed.

Cody was down in less than a minute. When he saw Carolyn and Lori seated in front of Helen's desk, he sent up a silent prayer that the problem wouldn't be major. The Circle T account was important to him. ''Good morning, Carolyn…Lori. How can I help you?''

Lori inspected him discreetly. She knew him only casually, but the general consensus among her female acquaintances was that the bank's new manager had, just by moving to town, improved the local scenery considerably. He was a good-looking devil, she conceded—tall, well-built, with gold-flecked brown hair, warm brown eyes and an ingratiating smile. Carolyn had commented once that Cody ''looks like a banker.'' Lori supposed that observation had been prompted by his impeccable dress and polished manner. He always looked so in control, self-assured perhaps to the point of being cocky. She couldn't imagine him ever being hot, sweaty, rumpled or unshaved.

And though she could count on the fingers of

one hand the times they had exchanged more than social pleasantries, he had made a few distinct impressions on her. One was that he probably wasn't an easy man to get to know well, a bit starched and dignified. Another was that he had an air of the hard-charging executive, a man who knew exactly where he wanted to go and how to get there. She couldn't help but admire a man with ambition since her ex-husband had been totally without it.

But Cody Hendricks also had the reputation of being a ladies' man. Lori had no idea if he was widowed, divorced or simply a confirmed bachelor, but gossip had it that he'd dated just about every eligible female for miles around. And that impression tended to cancel out the others. Having once been married to a man who'd chased women so hard for so long he'd been unable to stop even after he had a wife, Lori found a ladies' man to be the most undesirable type of all.

"You said there was a problem, Helen," Cody now said.

"Yes, sir." Helen seemed vastly relieved to be able to turn it over to him. "Carolyn came in this morning to transfer the money in a savings account to a certificate of deposit, but it seems her records indicate there is more money in the account than we show. The problem apparently lies in a withdrawal that she says she never made.''

"Surely there's a reasonable explanation for the discrepancy,'' he said confidently. "Never fear, Carolyn, we'll straighten this out in a few minutes. I'll get the file on the account. Why don't you and Lori wait in my office while I clear this up.'' Smiling affably, he held out an arm in invitation. Lori and Carolyn looked at each other, then stood and followed him into the main part of the lobby.

"You know where my office is, don't you?'' he asked. When Carolyn nodded, he said, "Good. Just go right in, and if you'd like coffee, my secretary will be happy to get some for you. I'll be right with you.'' He strode off like a man with an important mission.

Lori noticed that Carolyn didn't look at all appeased. She didn't blame her. It was disconcerting to discover funds missing from one's bank account. "Come on, Caro,'' she said reassuringly. "You know it will be taken care of.''

Suddenly something dawned on her, and she turned to her cousin, eyes widening. "Good grief! Hank is eerie, isn't he? Absolutely unbelievable.''

"I know,'' Carolyn said. "Anything he tells me from now on, no matter how ridiculous, is fact as far as I'm concerned.''

The women took a winding staircase to the mezzanine. Cody's office was at the end of the carpeted corridor. The woman at the desk in the reception room greeted them, and when they told her they were to wait for Mr. Hendricks, she showed them into his private inner sanctum.

The room was exactly what Lori imagined a successful executive's office would be. Done in shades of green and burgundy, the furnishings were expensive and completely masculine. His oversize oak desk dominated the room; in front of it stood a grouping of burgundy leather chairs. The heels of her pumps sank into the forest-green carpet. She and Carolyn took two of the chairs facing the desk and waited.

They did not have to wait long. Cody joined them in only a few minutes, carrying a computer printout in his hand. He was studying it, shaking his head and frowning. "Carolyn, Helen was right. Our records do show a two-thousand-dollar withdrawal on October 13. Is it possible you simply forgot about it?"

Carolyn uttered a little laugh. "I'm afraid I'm not so well off that I would forget two thousand dollars, Cody. And I know Lori wouldn't, either. That withdrawal was not made, at least not by us."

Cody rounded the desk and sat down in his

chair. "This doesn't look familiar to you?" He shoved a small slip of paper across the desk. Carolyn leaned forward and took it, studied it, then handed it to Lori. "No," she said firmly.

Lori saw it was a withdrawal slip. She shook her head. "We didn't make this transaction. I keep Carolyn's books and reconcile all her statements." She glanced up at Cody. "And I'm *very* meticulous."

"I want this straightened out, Cody," Carolyn said a bit irritably.

"So do I." He sat back and tapped his chin thoughtfully. "So do I." He lapsed into silence for a minute, lost in thought; then he sat up. "Well, it's the bank's problem, not yours. I'll okay the transfer of your entire account, including the two thousand. Then it'll be up to us to find the misplaced money."

"Can you do that?" Lori asked in surprise.

Cody nodded. Taking Carolyn's word for it was good banking procedure. The Circle T account was far more important to the bank than two thousand dollars. "Yes," he said. "It's what we call an acceptable risk, and acceptable risks are what banking's all about."

"Thank heavens," Carolyn said with relief.

"I'm really sorry for the trouble."

"I just hope you find the money," Lori remarked. As an accountant, she knew a misplaced dime could sometimes drive her crazy.

"Oh, we'll find it," Cody said with a charming smile and more confidence than he actually felt.

"How can you be so sure?" she asked.

"I'm not entirely without experience in this sort of thing. I'm betting it turns out to be nothing more serious than a clerical error." Cody wished he believed that, but he didn't for a minute. Something like this could turn out to be a real bag of worms. But treating the matter casually would lessen its importance to the two women. Hopefully they would quickly forget the episode and not mention it to anyone. He wanted to handle this in house and as quietly as possible. "By the way, Carolyn, does anyone else have access to the account?"

"Only Lori. She's on all my accounts. It saves me from having to run into town for every little thing."

"I see."

The expression on his face did not alter, but something in the tone of his voice made Lori flinch.

"Cody, I really want to thank you for believing me," Carolyn said.

"Of course I believe you. I'll call Helen and

her to complete the transfer of funds. Again, I apologize for the delay.''

Carolyn and Lori both stood up, so he did, too. Carolyn offered her hand. ''Please don't apologize. You've been most accommodating. I hope this doesn't turn out to be a real problem for you.''

''I fully expect to have it cleared up before the day's over.'' He turned to Lori. ''Goodbye, Lori. I hope to see you again soon.''

A few parting pleasantries were exchanged, then the women left. Cody stared after them, and Lori's lovely face lingered in his mind. Getting to know her better was so tempting. He wished he knew if the coach was still in the picture; it had been some time since he'd seen them together. He supposed he could ask her to have coffee with him next Monday when she came into the bank. Even if she was romantically involved, there wouldn't be anything wrong with that. If she accepted, he could pump her for details about her private life.

But for now, he had something serious to contend with. Sitting down, he mulled over his problem. He was surprised that an astute businesswoman like Carolyn would have had money tied up in a passbook savings account, let alone have left it untouched for years. Interest on such accounts was pitiful, and statements were issued only twice a year instead of every month.

Yet that might be in their favor now. Statements were due to go out the end of December. Whoever took the money had to know that and be getting nervous. Sometimes nervous people tipped their hand.

Cody studied the withdrawal slip before him. The handwritten signature in the upper right-hand corner was his starting point. Southwest's policy was to have their tellers sign or initial every deposit or withdrawal they handled, for this very reason. If a transaction was questionable, he knew exactly whom to go to. This slip was signed "Debbie." He punched the intercom, and his secretary answered. "Martha, I'd like to see all the morning's deposits and withdrawals."

"Yes, sir. I'll have them for you in a few minutes."

The request was a normal one and wouldn't raise so much as an eyebrow. As manager, Cody routinely asked to see the transactions, just to get a feel for the amount of money flowing into and out of the bank. This morning, however, when Martha brought the slips of paper to him, he barely glanced at the figures. His interest was all on the signatures in the right-hand corner, and something caught his attention right away.

The only Debbie working for the bank was Debbie Sue Watson, and there were dozens of slips with DSW written on them in a neat, feminine script, but not one was signed "Debbie." Of course it was possible that Debbie might have forgotten and signed rather than initialed one slip, but he didn't think so. In training, tellers were cautioned time and time again to sign their transactions exactly the same way every time, and it soon became habit.

Instinct told Cody what had happened to Carolyn's account. A dormant account, a teller—or somebody—desperately needing money, a withdrawal slip signed with another teller's name. The thief simply hadn't known that Debbie Watson initialed rather than signed her transactions. Fortunately, embezzlers always slipped up one way or another. Unfortunately, he didn't know if this slip-up would help him or not.

Again he punched the intercom, this time to get in touch with Ralph Gainey, his executive assistant. "Good morning, Cody."

"Good morning, Ralph. I'm afraid what I'm going to ask of you isn't going to make me the most popular man in Crystal Creek today."

"Leave it to me, boss. I'll run interference for you. What is it?"

"I want you to get in touch with the key staff— Claude, Joe, Florence, and Chip. Tell them to be prepared to stay after the doors close this afternoon, and I'm afraid there might be some burning of the midnight oil. I'm sorry, but it can't be helped."

"Good as done," Ralph said. "Want me to tell them anything else?"

"No. I'll explain when we meet in my office."

"Fine. See you then."

Cody depressed the button, looked up and sighed. These things were damnably touchy. Embezzlement always involved a fellow worker, and that made it impossible to remain completely dispassionate. Catching an employee with a hand in the till or wringing a confession out of a jumpy, scared one was not one of the pleasant aspects of his job.

But if he didn't trace the missing money an official audit eventually would uncover the loss and ask some questions. And the answers naturally would be dispatched to corporate headquarters. So he had to get to the bottom of it here, as quickly and quietly as possible, long before a whisper of it reached Houston and the ears of DeWitt Hendricks, Southwest's CEO...and Cody's father.

CHAPTER THREE

SINCE LORI and Carolyn had other errands to run in town, they didn't return to the ranch until noon. As Cody had hoped, his casual dismissing of the theft as a bookkeeping error had the effect of almost erasing the episode from their minds. Their only comments on the subject during the drive from town centered on Hank's incredible clairvoyant powers.

As soon as she dropped Carolyn off in front of the main house, Lori went straight to her own place, where she changed into jeans and a sweatshirt, her working uniform. She cast a woeful look in the direction of the desk in her bedroom. From now until the end of the year she fully expected to be one busy woman, and she would start today with Homer Thornton's taxes. He was the nervous type who liked getting them paid early.

She quickly ate a sandwich and drank a diet cola, then went to work. By four-thirty she had finished her task. Normally she would have phoned

Homer and had him pick up the paperwork. But this afternoon she decided to deliver the material to his ranch because his place was near the Double Bar, Brock Munroe's spread, and Lori wanted to see Amanda Walker, who was spending a lot of time at the Double Bar these days. When she wasn't at her own place in Austin, she was here. Every time Lori was around Amanda and Brock she could hear wedding bells in the distance. She was a little surprised that the nuptials had not already taken place, but they were so absorbed in the renovation of Brock's wonderful old ranch house that she assumed they just hadn't found the time to tie the knot.

The renovation project was the main reason Lori wanted to pay them a visit. It was hard not to get interested in watching a grand house come to life again. Having recently been through such a project, admittedly on a much smaller scale, Lori had been glad to give them the benefit of her limited expertise. Amanda declared she had been a world of help, though it seemed to Lori all she'd done was warn them of the disappointments and delays they were bound to encounter. She wouldn't have dreamed of giving Amanda decorating advice. The woman, a personal shopper by trade, epitomized style and taste and needed no one's advice, but Lori enjoyed watching the project take shape.

After dropping off Homer's papers and spending a few minutes chatting with his wife, she drove to the Munroe ranch and found Amanda sitting on a back porch step, sanding a strip of molding. She was dressed in old jeans, disreputable sneakers and a floppy shirt, but not even the clothes, the smudges on her face and sawdust in her hair could detract from Amanda's beauty.

"Well, hello, friend," Amanda greeted her brightly. "Pull up a step, grab a sheet of sandpaper and make yourself at home."

Lori sat down and leaned against the porch railing. No sooner had she gotten comfortable than she was accosted by Alvin, Brock's homely, shaggy dog. She had heard that Alvin was by nature lazy and antisocial, but he always greeted her when she came to the ranch. He didn't leap into the air and bark joyously by any means, but at least he always put in an appearance to acknowledge her presence. "Hello, Alvin," she said and reached behind one of his ears to scratch gently. The dog tolerated that for a minute, then ambled off to stretch out on the porch and keep a watchful eye on the two women.

"Look at this wood," Amanda said, holding out

the strip of molding she had been working on. "Isn't it beautiful?"

"It certainly is," Lori said admiringly.

"I must have stripped five coats of paint off it. I often wonder what compels people to paint over beautiful wood. I'm not even going to stain it. Varnish, that's all. So far every strip of wood in the house matches every other strip perfectly. Brock has a treasure here, a house that was built to last generations."

"I know. But I think he has an even greater treasure in finding someone who loves the house the way you do and is willing to put in all these tedious hours."

Amanda smiled almost dreamily. "And I do love it. Oh, Lori, I never thought I'd have anything like this! When I think of the chrome and glass and modern art I used to surround myself with... Now I'm searching for deacon's benches and trestle tables and pie safes. I've changed...a lot."

"Speaking of change, I ran into Mary Gibson in town the other day. She looks fantastic! You did wonders for her, Amanda."

"Oh...she just needed some self-confidence and a shove in the right direction."

"You're being modest. I sure wish you could do the same for me."

Amanda turned her head and stared at Lori. "You? But, Lori, you're an extremely pretty woman. You wear lovely clothes, and you wear them extremely well. Mary, bless her heart, was…well, rather dowdy when I took her in tow."

"Sometimes I feel I'm borderline dowdy."

"Wrong," Amanda insisted. "But if you feel that way, you probably need some kind of change." Amanda studied her a minute. "You know what I think—a perm would do wonders for you. I can just see you with a mass of curls all over your head. It would look great."

Lori's hair was thick, dark brown and had just enough natural wave to it that she'd never felt it necessary to do much but have it cut occasionally and tuck under the ends with a curling iron. Now she reached up and ran her fingers through it. "You really think so?"

"I know so. Trust me. It would give you a whole new look. I'm often amazed at what a simple change in hairstyle can do for a woman."

At that moment the back door swung open and the heavy tread of boot heels sounded across the wooden porch. Lori glanced over her shoulder, expecting to see Brock. Instead, a dark-haired, mustached cowboy stood in the center of the porch, holding half a dozen empty paint cans. "All right if I put these in the back of the pickup, Amanda? I can carry them off tomorrow.''

"Yes, that's fine," Amanda said.

The man nodded in Lori's direction, then climbed down the steps and ambled off across the yard. Lori watched him, frowning. She waited until she was sure he was out of hearing range before turning to Amanda. "Luke Harte?" she asked incredulously.

Amanda nodded and pulled a face.

"Is he working for Brock now?"

Another nod. "I hate it, I really do. I just don't like the man, and I'm not even sure why. But we had to have somebody, and Luke seemed to be the only one available. Mary had to let him go, you know."

"Yes, I'd heard. Because of the talk?"

"Uh-huh. It embarrassed poor Mary to death, but I think what she found even more embarrassing was getting herself into a position to cause talk."

"How was she to know, Amanda? A woman living alone on that ranch, trying to get her ostrich-breeding operation off the ground, with a husband in jail! Of course she needed help. I'm sure it never occurred to her that hiring a cowboy half her age would start lips flapping. I'm surprised the people around here didn't realize that and keep their mouths shut. Sometimes the Crystal Creek grapevine irritates me to death.''

''People are going to talk, Lori,'' Amanda said with a sigh. ''Always have and always will. You know that. And the abrupt change in Mary's appearance... Well, people were convinced Luke was the reason behind it.''

Lori nodded distractedly. Her gaze, almost of its own volition, wandered to Luke Harte, who was stashing the paint cans in the back of Brock's pickup. She knew Luke mainly by reputation, and it wasn't a good one. Devilishly handsome, the young cowboy had worked several of the area ranches. Vernon, who was a good friend of Brock's, had made several remarks about Luke that led Lori to believe Carolyn's husband had no use for Luke whatsoever. The first time Lori had met him, he'd looked at her with an air of arrogance that she had found insufferable. She had heard him described as a ''smooth-talking drifter with an eye for the ladies.'' She had no idea why she remembered that since Luke Harte was of absolutely no concern to her and never would be.

Amanda rubbed her hand over the piece of wood she held and smiled with satisfaction. ''Smooth as a baby's butt. One down and umpteen to go.'' Standing, she said, ''Brock's up in the attic unearthing all sorts of goodies. Let's go see what he's found.''

''Sounds great. I want to see what all you've done since I was last here.'' Lori jumped to her feet.

''I put chili in the slow cooker this morning. Stay for supper?''

''I'd love to.''

SOUTHWEST BANK closed its doors for business at four o'clock. Tellers immediately began reconciling their cash drawers, locking them and carrying them to the vault. By the time five o'clock rolled around, most of the employees had left the building. The executive offices on the mezzanine, however, were buzzing with activity. Cody and five of his officers had gathered in his office. Coats had come off, ties were loosened, sleeves were rolled to the elbow. Everyone was curious about the unusual meeting.

''I want to apologize,'' Cody began, ''for unhappy spouses, broken dinner engagements, 'Monday Night Football,' and anything else I've fouled up tonight. But something came up this morning that I'd like to get to the bottom of as quickly as possible.'' Succinctly he told them about the episode with Carolyn's account. ''Frankly, dormant accounts are a mystery to me, but all banks have them, and they're the prime targets for embezzlers.''

The very word *embezzler* caused a murmur to ripple through the small gathering, but no one said anything. Cody continued. ''What we're going to do tonight is investigate the checking and savings accounts of everyone who works at this bank, going back to…oh, June, and we're also going to look at all dormant accounts. I'll do those. I know I could call Houston and get a team from Audit, but you know how those people operate. They come on like gangbusters, and that would cause a lot of talk. I want to keep this as quiet as I can.''

Florence Nivens, the trust officer, spoke up. ''Cody, I've never done anything like this before. What will we be looking for?''

''Anything that smacks of financial trouble.''

''Like what?''

''Oh, for instance, if someone's borrowed to the maximum from this branch, go back over their checking account and look for a monthly payment to a loan company…or several loan companies. Anyone who would pay those exorbitant interest rates when this bank offers them a rock-bottom one probably has money troubles. Just flag any file that bothers you. Okay?''

Members of the group glanced from one to the other, nodding a little uncertainly. "Good," Cody said. "Now we'll go downstairs and get those files."

It was a tedious task, taking hours to complete. At seven o'clock, Chip Larsen, the assistant loan officer, went over to the Longhorn Coffee Shop and returned with sandwiches and drinks. By nine-thirty everyone had assembled back in Cody's office. He looked over the group. "Well, anybody have anything? Ralph?"

His assistant shook his head. "Nothing. A couple of chronic overdrafters, but the overdrafts have always been made up. All in all, my bunch seems to be a pretty fiscally responsible bunch."

"Florence?"

"Same here, Cody. Overdrafts were as big as it got. I found only one employee who has borrowed to the limit from us, and the loan's being paid off right on schedule. No payments to loan companies."

Cody heard variations on that theme from everyone in the group. No one found anything unusual or alarming in the files. He could barely swallow his disappointment.

"What about the dormant accounts?" Ralph asked.

Cody shook his head. "Mrs. Trent's account was the only one showing any activity since June." He looked away a minute, then heaved a sigh. "Well, we did our best. I can't thank you all enough for your time. Just leave your files here on my desk. They can go back in the morning. It's late enough as it is. I'm sure I don't need to stress the importance of keeping this quiet."

When everyone had left, he stared morosely at the stack of folders on his desk. The answer to the theft wasn't in there, and he had been so sure it would be.

Cody's thoughts turned to the tellers. They were the ones who handled large amounts of cash every day, and they were the ones most familiar with the procedures involving deposits and withdrawals. Two thousand dollars and not a penny more. That alone arrested his attention. Embezzlers were usually greedier than that. Maybe this incident had been a one-time emergency.

So if the answer wasn't in those bank accounts, he would have to dig deeper. Into his employees' private lives. One of them had a problem; he was sure of it.

Motive, he thought. *Find the motive and you'll find the thief.*

CHAPTER FOUR

LORI SPENT most of the following week on her accounts, making a considerable dent in her work-
load. But on Friday she went to the beauty shop
and got the first perm of her life. The effect startled
her—a mass of dark brown ringlets, spritzed and
fluffed until she looked as though she had pounds
of hair. But after she got home and studied herself
in the mirror a dozen times, she decided she liked
it. At least it was a change, although just what she
was changing for she couldn't imagine.

On Saturday morning she was up and about
early, ready for a drive to Austin. Staring at her
reflection in the mirror, she grinned. She was wearing one of the few new outfits she had bought recently—a siren-red split skirt with matching
cropped top and slender suede boots. Long gold
earrings dangled from her lobes. The once sleek
cap of dark hair was now a mass of curls. The
woman staring back at her was nothing at all like

the Lori Porter she knew, and that suited her just fine.

As she got in her car, she spied Carolyn coming out of the house and heading for her. Lori waved.

"Is it absolutely necessary to get up at dawn for the book fair?"

"If you don't get there early, the locals get all the real good stuff."

"God, you sci-fi freaks are all nuts."

"Hey, different strokes, you know."

Carolyn studied her. "Lori, you look great! Is that a new outfit?"

"Yes. Like it?"

"I love it. And you've curled your hair."

"Got a perm, actually."

"It suits you. You really do look great."

"Thanks, Caro."

"Have a good time. Hope you find something."

"So do I."

Lori drove through the front gate and headed for town, then east to Austin. It was a glorious sun-filled day, the kind that made her remember why fall was her favorite time of the year. And if the weather and her new look weren't enough, the Galaxy Book Fair always got her in high spirits, as it did all the science fiction "nuts" who flocked to it every year.

From modest beginnings, the fair had grown to such huge proportions that it now occupied a ballroom and two meeting rooms in one of Austin's luxury hotels. When Lori arrived, she found the rooms already packed with people. Publishing houses had set up booths to advertise their new releases, and booksellers came by the dozens. Most of the attendees, however, were simply fans like Lori who had come to pore over the used-book stalls, hoping to find an out-of-print book to add to their collections. Some of them got into the spirit of the occasion by dressing up like favorite characters from favorite books. The costumes always were clever, completely bizarre and great fun to see. They certainly added a colorful note to proceedings that consisted mainly of people from all walks of life rifling through piles of musty books with the seriousness of archaeologists studying ancient ruins.

Lori's own book collection was so extensive that she found it harder and harder every year to stumble onto a valuable acquisition. She had about decided she would go away empty-handed today when her eyes fell on a book that was partially obscured by another. Reaching down, she picked it up, and her eyes widened. *Another Sea* by Jack Dirdyea. She carefully opened the delicate, yellowed little paperback to the copyright page. 1966! She couldn't believe it! Why hadn't a treasure like this been snapped up long ago?

She looked at the man behind the table. He was smiling at her knowingly. She could tell he was a pro, not simply a collector who had brought in a few items to sell or swap, but someone who devoted all his time to acquiring books to sell for an enormous profit. "How much?" she asked.

"A hundred," he replied briskly.

Lori's mouth fell. Of course the books rose in value as the years passed, but one hundred dollars? The man was unconscionable. Now she understood why the book was still available. "That's a bit steep, don't you think?"

The man shrugged. "I spent a year running that thing down, and my time's worth something, y'know. Finally found it in a farmhouse in Connecticut. It's the only one here today. I've checked. The price has gone up since Dirdyea died."

Lori stared at the book in her hand. It was a real find, an early work by a man who had gone on to be a master of the genre. The price was outrageous, but she couldn't seem to put the book down. She was vaguely aware that someone was standing behind her, probably someone who would snatch it up if she laid it down, and she knew the chances were slim that she would ever find a '66 Dirdyea again.

But the sensible side of her nature prevailed. It was ridiculous of her to even consider buying it. Uttering a little sigh of regret, she made a move to put the book back on the table, but to her astonishment, a strong masculine hand curled around her wrist. She gasped.

"If you buy it, will you let me read it?"

She turned...and gasped again. "Cody!"

Cody grinned at her. "It took me a full five minutes to recognize you. You've done something to your hair." His hand was still wrapped firmly around her wrist.

"What are you doing here?" Lori cried.

"Isn't that funny? That was exactly my first thought when *I* saw *you.* I had to see what you were up to. When I saw the book you were looking at so covetously, I had my answer. You're one of us."

"You're a sci-fi buff?"

"I think 'nut' is the correct term."

Lori laughed. "I'm sorry...it doesn't fit. It just doesn't."

"So I've been told. I might say the same for you." Cody tapped the cover of the book she held.

"I'm going to warn you—if you don't buy it, I will. The price is only going to go up."

"Do you really think so?" she asked, glancing uncertainly at the book.

"I'd bet on it."

"Well…in that case…" She turned to the man behind the table; he had a cat-got-the-canary expression on his face. "Do you take checks?"

"Nope."

"I'm her banker," Cody said. "Her check's good."

"I don't care who you are, pal. I don't take checks."

Lori sighed, reached into her handbag and withdrew two fifty-dollar bills from her wallet. "You're right, Cody. Nut *is* the word." Handing the bills to the man, she pocketed her treasure.

Cody slipped a hand under her elbow as they moved away. "Have you had breakfast?"

"No. I wanted to get here early."

"Same with me. Since you're considerably poorer than you were a minute ago, it's my treat."

By now it was late for the breakfast crowd, so the rotunda restaurant just off the hotel's main lobby was almost deserted. After being served coffee and ordering, Lori and Cody simply looked at each other a minute, then laughed simultaneously.

Cody opened his mouth to say something, but at that moment a woman walked by their table. She was dressed in a pink sequined bodysuit with enormous pink wings at each shoulder. Her hair had been sprayed pink and moussed to stand out from her head in spikes. "Tell me who she's dressed like," he said to Lori with a grin.

"Let me see... Oh, I know. Princess Cerisa, daughter of Viktor, the overseer of the planet's deadliest hunting grounds. *Twilight of the Lost World.* Right?"

"Right," he said admiringly. "I've found a soul mate. You'll have to pay me a visit and see my collection."

"Love to." Lori wondered if that ever would actually come to pass.

"Do you believe in UFOs?" Cody asked.

"Of course. Every time I hear one's been sighted, I always wonder where it's from."

Cody smiled. "So do I. And, Lori, real bankers, *good* bankers aren't supposed to believe in UFOs."

Lori chuckled. "I know. Neither are good accountants." She lifted the cup to her lips and stared at him over its rim. He looked so different this morning without his customary natty business suit. He wore cords, a velour shirt and loafers. The clothes transformed him in some indefinable way, making him look younger and less the hard-charging executive. More approachable, she guessed.

"Have you always lived in Crystal Creek?" Cody asked.

Lori shook her head. "I've only been there five years. I grew up in San Antonio, a city girl through and through."

"What took you to the boondocks?"

"A divorce, unfortunately. When Caro heard about it, she insisted I come and stay with her for a while. It sounded appealing. I expected to stay maybe a month. I didn't think I was cut out for the country life."

"But now?"

"It grows on you. I've met a lot of people, and I have my business. What about you? You're from a big city."

Cody looked surprised. "How did you know that?"

"Cody, you know the kind of town Crystal Creek is. Somebody's aunt's cat can't have kittens without half the town knowing about it an hour later. You're from...let's see...Houston, right?"

"Right."

"So, what was your first impression of Crystal Creek?"

"That it was a burg."

"And now?"

"I like it. I really do."

"It's the pace, don't you think?" Lori remarked. "At first it drove me crazy that no one ever seemed to care if things got done today, tomorrow or next week. But I've slowed down, too. I'm afraid a city would drive me crazy these days."

Their food arrived, and for a few minutes conversation was put on hold. Then Cody asked, "Do you go back to San Antonio often?"

"Frequently. My mother and grandmother are there."

"Are they all the family you have?"

"There's Caro, of course, and Beverly. And Uncle Francis, who lives with Mom and Grandma. Plus a couple of other uncles I never see. They live on the East Coast. Uncle Francis is with an insurance company. My mom teaches school and has for forty-two years. Grandma cooks…constantly, incessantly. When she isn't cooking, she's force-feeding everyone in sight."

Cody smiled. "Sounds like a nice family, but somehow I thought you were related to J.T. McKinney."

Lori smiled and shook her head. "No, not by blood. Caro's sister was J.T.'s first wife, so Beverly is a cousin to J.T.'s kids. Somehow we all seem to be family."

"No kids of your own?"

"No. I used to regret that, but considering the way things turned out for Michael and me, perhaps it's best. What about you? Family?"

"Yes, father, mother, brother and sister."

"All in Houston?"

"All in Houston."

Lori waited, expecting to hear a little something more about his family. What line of work his father was in, for instance, but nothing was forthcoming and she was disappointed. The man across the table from her was rapidly becoming more than the rather stuffy banker Cody Hendricks had always seemed to be. Dozens of questions popped into her head. She was never sure how much questioning was considered polite interest and how much was plain nosiness, but since she really was interested in finding out more about him, she plunged ahead. "Have you ever been married? Any kids?"

He shook his head slowly. "I was married once when I was in my early twenties. We were high school sweethearts. We had been together ten years when she died. Leukemia."

"Oh…I'm…so sorry."

"We never had kids. She was sick a long time."

Cody noticed how Lori's eyelashes dipped. The question she had asked always cast a pall over conversation, and that was the main reason he hated it to be asked. He was relieved now it was out in the open and wouldn't be mentioned again.

Lori was tackling her food with seriousness, wondering, no doubt, how to get the easy talk started up again. Lord, she looked so different today, and it was more than the hair, though the style did wonders for her. She didn't seem so cool and reserved. A sci-fi fan, of all things! He wondered if the book fair was the only reason she was in Austin today. Coach Chaney was here now; perhaps she was meeting him later.

Well, there was only one way to find out. A woman who could instantly identify Princess Cerisa and *Twilight of the Lost World* was not someone he was apt to run into every day of the week. She had always intrigued him; this morning she fascinated him. If possible, he had to get to know her better.

"So, now that it has been established that we're both sci-fi fanatics, one more test. How do you feel about Hill Country barbecue?"

"Only that it's the very best in the entire world."

"Good. You passed. This means we'll have to continue seeing each other. How would you like to drive to Llano Monday night for some of the best of the best?"

Lori was a little surprised by the invitation. He'd been in Crystal Creek six months and had never asked her out before. In fact, if gossip could be believed, she was probably the only eligible woman who hadn't had even one date with him. What had made Cody notice her now? Could clothes and a new hairdo really make that much of a difference? Was it their common interest in science fiction? Who cared? "Why, I'd love to, Cody. Thanks."

Scratch the coach, he thought with satisfaction. This was turning out to be one of the most pleasant mornings of his life.

They finished breakfast, had another cup of coffee and talked about nothing in particular—his work, her work, Crystal Creek gossip. But Lori noticed something—the one thing he didn't talk about was himself. No boyhood reminiscences peppered the conversation, and only once did he mention his family. That was when she asked him what had made him take up banking in the first place. He'd merely shrugged and said, "There've always been bankers in the family." Nevertheless, by the time they left the restaurant, she clearly felt the fragile beginnings of a friendship.

They spent another hour or so at the fair, browsing through books, discussing the ones they'd both read and their favorite authors. Cody made a couple of purchases, but Lori decided that her hundred-dollar Dirdyea was her limit for that year.

Finally, Cody looked at his watch. "I'm enjoying the heck out of this, Lori, but unfortunately, I have to be going. Some old friends invited me to spend the weekend at their house on Lake Travis, and they'll be waiting. I guess I'll spend this afternoon fishing."

Lori experienced a twinge of disappointment, which was pretty silly when she thought about it. "Have a good time. Hope you catch lots."

"Catching fish isn't really the point of it all." Grinning, he reached for her hand and held it in his. "The Force be with you."

"And with you."

"See you Monday night. Say, seven?"

"Seven's fine. I'm looking forward to it. By the way, Cody…the money that was missing from Carolyn's account. Did you find it?"

Hedging, he simply gave her the A-OK sign with his thumb and forefinger.

"That's good."

He gave her hand a little shake, then walked off, hands in pockets, whistling. Lori stared after him, a small smile touching her lips. She was beginning to think the man she'd just had breakfast with was the real Cody Hendricks, a man who enjoyed escapist reading and fishing, that perhaps the dignified banker was the facade. She also realized that Monday night's date was the first thing she had really looked forward to in a long time.

LORI WAS ONE of the first customers in Southwest Bank when it opened its doors Monday morning, and there was no one ahead of her at Mary Alice's cage.

"Good morning, Mary Alice."

"Hi, Lori. Love your hair! Mama said you were in the shop Friday. Yeah, I really like that."

"Thanks." Lori watched as the teller took care of her transaction. "By the way, I'm going to be running errands most of the morning. If you don't have other plans, why don't we have lunch together?"

Mary Alice's smile was radiant. "Thanks, Lori.

I'd like that. Do you mind waiting until a quarter to one?''

"Not a bit. We'll miss the heaviest crowd then. I'll wait for you out front.''

"Thanks. Here you go.''

Mary Alice shoved the deposit slip toward her. Lori put it in her bag, turned and went out the entrance doors. Outside, she all but collided with Cody who was coming up the steps.

"Well, good morning,'' he greeted brightly.

"Good morning.'' He was back in his dignified banker mode, Lori noticed. Dark suit, crisp shirt, subdued tie. She didn't think she had ever known a man who wore clothes so beautifully. "How was your weekend?''

"Gloriously macho. Lots of beer, fried fish and tall tales. How was *Another Sea?*''

"Wonderful. Not as complex as his later stuff but highly entertaining. And, yes, you may borrow it. I'll give it to you tonight.''

"Thanks.''

"You realize, of course, that I would only loan that book to another collector.''

He nodded. "I promise, I'll treat it with the respect it deserves. As thanks, let me buy you lunch.''

"Oh, Cody, I'm sorry, but I'm having lunch with Mary Alice."

"Mary Alice Priest?"

"Yes."

"I've noticed you always go to her station. Is she a relative?"

He'd noticed that? "No, we're just friends."

"Then I suppose I'll have to settle for dinner tonight." His smile was dazzling. "I can hardly wait."

"See you at seven," Lori said, and with a jaunty little wave, she continued on down the steps toward her car.

He watched her, the movement of her hips under her slim skirt, the scissoring motion of her shapely legs as she crossed the drive, the bouncing of her dark curls in the sunshine. And he realized with something of a start that for the first time since coming to Crystal Creek, he had a date he was anticipating with a great deal of pleasure.

Cody turned and pushed open the entrance door, stepping aside to let a young woman pass. On his way to the stairs, he was halted several times by friends and acquaintances who wanted to chat. Then he went upstairs to his office.

"Anything hanging fire, Martha?" he asked as he entered the reception room.

"Nothing. Mayor Avery called, but he said it wasn't important, that he'd catch you later."

Cody nodded and pushed open the door to his office. Once he was seated behind his desk, he pulled a legal pad out of the center drawer and studied the scribbled notes he'd written on it. They contained everything he had been able to learn, through discreet inquiries here and there, about the personal lives of the bank employees who handled money. Unfortunately, the notes hadn't yielded any more valuable information than the financial histories had.

His eyes fell on the very last notation. *Mary Alice Priest—25, lives with mother, a manicurist, M.A. main breadwinner, shy, no info on friends, hobbies or outside interests, remarkable work attendance record, no credit info.*

He knew less about Mary Alice than he did about anyone at the bank. It was as though she left work every afternoon, went home and wasn't seen or heard of again until she walked through the bank's front door the next morning. Nothing wrong with that, of course, but it did make her stand out from the crowd. Most of the employees were civic-minded, active in a number of things, and their lives seemed to be open books.

He recalled the few times he'd had occasion to

speak to Mary Alice. The employees usually enjoyed it when the boss stopped for a chat, but not her. She always looked as if she wished the floor would open up and swallow her, and she never managed anything but monosyllabic answers to his questions. Several times he had spotted her alone in the break room, her head buried in a book. He had seen employees going off to lunch in laughing groups, but he didn't recall ever seeing Mary Alice with them.

But apparently she had one friend—Lori. Perhaps tonight he could think of a way to bring Mary Alice into the conversation and learn a little more about the young teller's private life.

Cody realized this affair with the missing money was becoming something of an obsession with him. Two thousand dollars wasn't all that much money. It wasn't enough to get the FBI interested, for instance. But it *was* enough to make Cody's actions questionable. Why, bank examiners might ask, had he so readily taken Carolyn's word that she hadn't made the withdrawal? Why hadn't he been more suspicious?

It would be almost impossible to explain to his father, who was so far up the ladder (and so out of touch with reality, to Cody's notion) that no one but the board of directors and presidents of huge corporations could get in to see DeWitt Hendricks without running a gauntlet of receptionists, secretaries and assistants. Unlike him, Cody dealt with real people whom he knew and lived close to. He didn't lend money to corporations; he lent money to people. Ninety-five percent of the time his customers could get in to see him without an appointment. But his father didn't understand that. Cody had caught plenty of flak over lending money to Mary Gibson to raise ostriches. His father considered the loan a risky one. Cody didn't want to have to turn around less than a month later and explain why he had turned over two thousand unaccounted-for dollars to a depositor.

Cody's relationship with his father had always been strained even though he knew no one he admired more than DeWitt Hendricks. As a young man he had chafed at the complicated set of rules, regulations and obligations DeWitt had imposed on the family, choosing rock climbing over golf, motorcycles over sailing, the University of Texas over Harvard. His older brother, Robert, was a chip off the old block, who thrived on being a Hendricks. His sister, Amy, was a free spirit who had become an accomplished commercial photographer, but even she adhered strictly to the family code of conduct.

That was why Crystal Creek was such a relief for Cody. Here no one had the slightest idea who his father was, and he wanted to keep it that way. For that reason he lived as he imagined a small town banker would. He rented a very nice but unpretentious house. He drove a dark blue sedan. His clothes were expensive but off the rack. Fortunately, the name Hendricks was so common that even if his father's name were mentioned, it would be a rare person who would make a connection between them. Cody seriously doubted there was a soul at the Crystal Creek branch who could name the CEO of the vast conglomerate. That made his interlude of anonymity easier. The last thing he wanted was for his employees and acquaintances to regard him as a rich man's son with a new toy.

Yet he knew this was nothing but an interlude. The day would come when his father would retire and Robert would become CEO. Then Cody would be expected to return to Houston and head the flagship branch. Legions of men would have been looking forward to that with great expectation, but he wasn't one of them.

Sighing, Cody made a tepee with his index fingers and rested his chin on it. There were any number of sound reasons for his wanting to solve the embezzlement himself. Whoever took the money had no right to it. Catching the thief would discourage others with sticky fingers. The banker in him liked neat books. But over and above all those reasons was the chief one—DeWitt Hendricks would expect nothing less.

THE HEAVY NOONTIME CROWD had begun to thin out when Lori and Mary Alice arrived at the Longhorn Coffee Shop. Lori steered her companion to a secluded booth in the rear of the popular eatery. After they had placed their orders, she folded her arms on the table and said, "So, Mary Alice, what's happening in your life?"

Apparently not much. Mary Alice mostly wanted to indulge in local gossip. "I hear they're turning the Double C Ranch into a winery," she said. "Can it be true?"

"It's Tyler who's going into wine making. J.T. says he wants it known that the ranch will always be the Double C Land and *Cattle* Company."

"I told Mama I bet it wasn't true. There's been a Double C Ranch all my life. Mrs. McKinney must be due to have her baby soon."

Lori nodded. "Any day now."

"She's so pretty."

"Cynthia? Yes, she is."

"When I first heard she was a Boston socialite

I figured she'd be a snob, but she isn't at all. She comes into the bank a lot, and she's just as nice as can be.''

''Isn't she, though?''

''Wasn't that just awful about Bubba Gibson? I mean, a rancher killing his own horses! I've heard he was in some kind of financial trouble. Is that right?''

''So I understand.''

''I saw Mrs. Gibson the other day. She looks so wonderful! I almost didn't recognize her.''

Lori smiled and nodded. ''Yes, the transformation is astonishing. But most of all, she's having a good time with her ostrich-breeding program. Everything is coming up roses for Mary these days, and it couldn't happen to a nicer person.''

That was the way the conversation went throughout lunch. Their dessert and coffee had been served when Mary Alice casually said, ''Did I tell you I have a steady boyfriend now?''

''No! Mary Alice, that's wonderful. Anyone I know?''

''I'm not sure. His name is Luke Harte.''

Lori hoped her expression didn't convey her dismay. Luke Harte? How could a shrinking violet like Mary Alice get tied up with someone like that?

Better still, why would a man with the reputation of a rake want to date such a timid woman?

"Oh?" Lori said, carefully measuring her voice and choosing her words. "How long have the two of you been going together?"

"Almost three months."

"Why haven't I heard about him before?"

Mary Alice smiled sheepishly. "To tell you the truth, Lori...I've only recently let myself believe Luke really is my *steady* boyfriend."

"How did you meet him?"

"He came in the bank a few times to cash his paycheck."

"Is it...serious?"

Mary Alice's eyes lit up. "I think, I *hope* we're going to get married soon. He's been talking about buying a ranch of his own as soon as he gets enough money saved up. Poor Luke's always had to work for the other fellow, but I just know someday he's going to have folks working for him. He'll have his own place and be a man of importance."

Luke Harte? Lori doubted it. Drifters didn't settle down, get married and buy a ranch. She didn't know why the news of Mary Alice's involvement with the man had her feeling so low. It was none of her business, and all she actually knew about Luke was gossip.

But none of the gossip was good. She thought about Mary Alice's nature, how badly she wanted to please and be liked, how easily she could be taken advantage of. And everything she'd ever heard about Luke described a man who took advantage of people whenever he could.

She looked at her companion. She didn't think she had ever seen Mary Alice looking so happy and animated. That only served to make Lori more uneasy.

Mary Alice then launched into a running patter about Luke and how wonderful he was. "He's saving every cent he can, so we don't go out much. Mostly he comes over to the house and we watch TV or rent a video. He loves Mama's cooking."

He sponges, Lori thought.

"And you know, Lori," Mary Alice enthused, "when Luke gets his place and we get married, he's going to have Mama live with us. Then she won't have to work with that bad back. Isn't that the sweetest thing you ever heard?"

Oh, God, it was too much! "I hope…everything works out nicely for you, Mary Alice. I really do." It was the best Lori could come up with.

"Thanks. Mama and I could use some good

luck, I'll tell you. Mama, especially. Seems like it's just been one bad thing after another for her. Isn't it awful that there are people in the world who never seem to have anything good happen to them? It'd just tickle me to death to let her sit a spell and do nothing but what she feels like doing.''

''That's nice.''

''Oh, we're very close. It's just been the two of us against the world for a long time.''

The waitress brought their check, which Lori picked up over Mary Alice's mild protest. The teller looked at her watch. ''Oh, darn, I've got to get back to work. I try never to be late. Mr. Hendricks doesn't like it, and I need that job. I don't know what Mom and I would do without it. But I wish I didn't have to get back. This has really been nice, Lori, lunch and all. I don't get a chance to do this sort of thing very often. Well…as a matter of fact, I *never* do unless you ask me. I don't know how to thank you.''

''Don't mention it. I enjoyed it, too. We'll do it again soon.''

It was only a few blocks from the Longhorn to the bank. Lori dropped Mary Alice off, then headed back to the Circle T. When she drove through the front gate, she spotted Vernon at the side of the house. She pulled the car up close and stuck her head out the window.

"Vern, just exactly what does Luke Harte do over at Brock's place?"

Vernon snorted. "As little as possible, it seems to me, but Brock and Amanda need an extra pair of hands, so I guess they'll keep him until they finish the house or they find someone else. Why on earth are you asking about Luke?"

"Because someone I know is sort of involved with him."

"Is the someone female?"

"Yes."

"If you like her, do her a big favor. Tell her to give him as wide a berth as possible."

"Why?"

"I don't trust him, and I can't put my finger on why I don't. But all my instincts tell me he's no good."

"Thanks," Lori said ruefully. "Be talking to you."

Deep in thought, she drove on and parked in front of her house. Her own instincts were working overtime, and they all urged her to tell Mary Alice that Luke Harte was bad news.

Lori's mother had often said that the reason Lori thought she had so many problems was that she tended to borrow those of others. She didn't seem to be able to help it. If she liked someone, she took on their burdens. Telling herself that Mary Alice was a grown woman who had to handle her own affairs did no good. All Lori could think about was—Luke the manipulator and Mary Alice the gullible. *She's so nice,* she thought. *Why doesn't the scoundrel leave her alone?*

But she was smart enough to know there was nothing she could do to warn Mary Alice since a woman in love usually had porridge for brains. So Lori decided she would try to forget the whole business, to concentrate instead on her date tonight…and on Cody Hendricks, who interested her far more than made good sense.

CHAPTER FIVE

MARY ALICE LEFT the bank at the usual time, four-thirty, and drove home after making a stop at the supermarket. Her car, a 1985 compact, needed new tires, but other than that, it was in superb condition. She had bought it from a widow who'd never had it out of town, and Mary Alice had religiously maintained it, no matter what the cost. The car, it seemed to her, represented her own life—neat, sensible, serviceable...and very, very ordinary.

As she carried her grocery sack into the house, she thought of Lori Porter. Lori epitomized everything Mary Alice wished she could be—beautiful, intelligent, self-assured. It was always such a thrill to be asked to lunch by someone like that. It made her feel important, and that didn't happen often. She guessed the last time was when Mr. Hendricks had presented her with an award for a year of perfect work attendance.

Inside the house, Mary Alice put the sack of groceries on the kitchen table and went to change clothes before making dinner for her mother and herself. The house, a 1970s three-bedroom model, was, like her car, kept in spotless condition inside, but the exterior needed so much work it boggled her mind to think about it. There was no way on earth she could ever put together enough money to pay for what needed doing unless she borrowed money from Southwest Bank, and that would mean a monthly payment forever. She had a meager savings account, but that she would never touch. The account and her car represented the only independence she had.

It seemed she had spent her entire life worrying about money. Occasionally she wondered what it would have been like to grow up in a two-parent family, to have a father who brought home a regular paycheck, maybe even to have gone to college. Not a big university, of course, but to a community college. Education beyond high school, she imagined, would have opened doors for her. But to regret it at this point was foolish. She had been with the bank since the summer after high school graduation, and until three months ago she would have bet she'd be there until she retired in forty years.

Now everything had changed. Every time Luke mentioned marriage and buying a ranch, she tingled inside. To get away from the sameness of her days, to leave her sensible house, sensible car, sensible job sounded like heaven.

Luke! What a change he had made in her life. Mary Alice still found it hard to believe he had chosen to date her when Crystal Creek was just full of women who would have given anything to be noticed by the handsome cowboy. ''I like the way your mind works, sugar,'' he once had told her, and she was sure he was the only man she'd ever known who had complimented her mind.

Luke was responsible for a lot of firsts in her life. He was the first to ever ask her out on a regular basis, the first to buy her a present, the first to make love to her. She no longer felt guilty about that, in spite of her strict Baptist upbringing. How could anything that made her feel so wonderful, so *wanted* be wrong? Besides, they were going to get married, weren't they? Luke had told her that made all the difference in the world, and she believed him. She always believed him. He had changed her life for good, and she would do anything for him. Hadn't she proved that over and over?

The front door opened and closed. ''Mary Alice, I'm home,'' her mother called.

Mary Alice sighed and fastened her jeans. She would fix supper, they would eat and then watch television, the same things they had done almost every night for as long as she could remember. The sameness of it was mind-numbing. But now there always was a chance Luke would call or come by. Six months ago she hadn't had anything to look forward to in the evening.

Oh, she did adore him so!

CODY WAS very punctual that evening. Lori was waiting in the living room of the ranch house. Carolyn and Vernon were having dinner with the McKinneys. Lori, of course, had been invited, too, but had begged off. When she'd explained about her date, Carolyn had said, "Cody Hendricks? Well, well."

"Now what's that supposed to mean?" Lori had demanded.

"Nothing. Just…well, well. Lori, I suppose you know Cody's considered *the* catch in these parts."

"Good grief, Caro. I haven't caught him. We're going out for barbecue."

At exactly seven o'clock the doorbell rang. Cody was so punctual that she wondered if he had been sitting out front for a few minutes, waiting for the appointed hour to arrive. Opening the door, she saw him standing in the soft glow of the porch light.

"Good evening," he said.

"Hello. Please come in."

He stepped into the foyer and glanced around. Then turning, he smiled. "Are you ready?"

"Yes, just let me get my jacket and handbag."

Their destination was Cooper's Barbecue in the small town of Llano, a twenty-minute drive from the ranch. Just driving up to the place made one hungry, for the aroma was irresistible. Inside, it was a typical barbecue joint. The pit man opened a sheet metal bin the size of a pickup bed, then waited for them to make their choice. Just about everything that could be barbecued was available—brisket, ribs, sausage, pork chops, chicken, even *cabrito* or young goat. The man pulled their selections off the grill, dipped the meat in sauce, then slapped it on butcher paper. They carried their food into an adjacent room and paid for it by the pound. Then they helped themselves to beans from a huge vat, bread, onions and chiles. By the time they finally sat down at one of the picnic tables in a back room, Lori was so hungry she felt faint.

Conversation while they ate was limited to small talk, reminiscences about other barbecue joints they had known and observations about the restaurant itself and the other patrons. Finally Lori looked down at a lone rib left on her plate. "I can't eat another bite,'' she moaned regretfully. ''The food is absolutely delicious.''

''How do you stay so slender with an appetite like that?''

''Genes, I guess. I don't always eat like this, however. But come to think of it, I ate pretty heartily at noon, too.''

Cody silently thanked her for bringing up lunch. He had been wondering how he was going to work Mary Alice into the conversation. ''How was your lunch date?''

''Oh, fine. Mary Alice is such a sweet person.''

''She's very shy, isn't she?''

Lori nodded. ''Extremely.''

''I make it my business to get to know most of the people at the bank, but Mary Alice shies away. I don't think she even attended the bank's Labor Day picnic.''

''I know, and it's such a shame. I think she'd like to be more outgoing but simply doesn't know how. From some of the things she's said I've gathered she and her mother have a tough time of it financially. Maybe she feels she can't compete with other women when it comes to clothes and that sort of thing.'' Lori paused and frowned. ''That's why I'm so upset over her choice of a boyfriend.''

"Oh?"

"She's seeing Luke Harte."

"Harte? Did he work for Mary Gibson for a while?"

"That's the one. Do you know him?"

"I don't really *know* him, no. I only saw him around Mary's place when we were hammering out the details of the ostrich-breeding operation."

"He's a cowboy, sort of a drifter. He works from place to place and never lasts long at any one of them. J.T. refused to have him work at the Double C. Now Luke's working for Brock Munroe, and Brock is a friend of Vern's. Vern doesn't have much good to say about Luke. The few times I've spoken to the man he acted sort of insolent. Of all people for Mary Alice to get involved with."

Cody took a sip of water. "She's a big girl, Lori."

"Not really. But I know what you mean—it's none of my business. Still…" Lori leaned forward and spoke earnestly. "Just think about it, Cody. Mary Alice is in her mid-twenties and still lives at home with her mother. I've never heard her mention friends, certainly not boyfriends. Yet, this painfully shy, and forgive me, rather mousy young thing captures the attention of a rakishly handsome cowboy who has her thinking about settling down on their own ranch. Luke can't keep a job for more than a few months. Where is a man like that going to get the money to buy a ranch?''

''Oh, I don't know. He could rob a bank.''

Cody had meant that as a joke, but the minute the words were out of his mouth, a thought formed in his head. Good Lord! He had been searching for something, *anything*. Could this be it? It was pretty thin, but he was pretty desperate.

''Very funny.'' Lori sighed sadly. ''I don't know why I've let this upset me. I guess it's because Mary Alice is so innocent and could so easily be taken advantage of. Sorry. I didn't mean to get carried away with this. You can't possibly be interested in any of it.''

''I think it's nice that you care so much. You probably make a hell of a good friend. But face it, Lori. If the girl is in love with a scoundrel, there's not a thing you can do about it.'' He glanced around, noticing that the restaurant had rapidly filled up. ''I guess we should let some of these folks have our table. Are you ready to go?''

''Yes.''

Cody tossed the butcher paper in a trash can and dropped the silverware in a sink, then held the door open for her. ''I just remembered something,'' he said as they drove away from the restaurant. ''The country club's Thanksgiving dance is tomorrow night. I hadn't planned to go, but if you'd go with me, it might be a lot of fun. I realize this is very short notice, but as I said, I hadn't planned to go.''

Lori had never been to the annual affair, but she seemed to recall hearing it was one of the year's swankiest events, not the sort of thing she was likely to be invited to. In fact, she could count on the fingers of one hand the times she had even been in the club during the past five years. But Cody doubtless would be in his rightful element. She briefly wondered if she would feel horribly out of place, then quickly dismissed the thought. She wasn't about to miss an opportunity to go out with him again.

''I'd love to go, Cody,'' she said. ''Thanks.''

Lori was feeling pleasantly relaxed. Cody was easy to be with, easy to talk to. He was completely free of pretense. He didn't waste any time trying to impress her. In fact, he was a surprise all the way around.

She twisted in the seat to look at him. ''How come you were sent to Crystal Creek, of all places?''

''I asked to be sent here.''

''You did?''

''You sound so surprised.''

"Well, it's just that... You must have worked at a very big bank in Houston."

"Southwest's flagship."

"Crystal Creek must have been quite a comedown."

"I didn't see it that way. Instead of working in just one department, here I run the bank from top to bottom."

Lori digested that. "Well, I guess that makes sense."

"And, too—big city banks impose all sorts of duties and rules and obligations on their officers. Most are ridiculous. Join *this* country club, attend *that* charity function. Individuality is not a priority at Southwest in Houston, I assure you."

"So you wanted to get away from the rat race," Lori said.

"Something like that."

When they arrived at the Circle T, Cody parked in front of the house. "You and your cousin must get along awfully well for you to live with her," he commented. "Right offhand, I can't think of a single relative I would want to live with."

"Well, Caro and I do get along famously, but I have my own place in back."

He opened his door. "Then I'll walk you to it."

"You don't have to do that, Cody. This ranch is the safest place on earth."

He rounded the car and opened the door for her. "No, my mom always told me to see my date to the door and safely inside."

"Well, I certainly wouldn't want you to disobey your mom," Lori said as she got out.

Cody took her arm, and they strolled around the side of the house to the small house in back. "This is a nice setup, Lori," he said when he saw the neat little structure.

"I enjoy it." She reached in her handbag for her key and shoved it in the lock. "Oh, I almost forgot. Come inside a minute. I have something for you."

Cody followed her inside. "Wait right here," she said and crossed the living room to go into what he could see was a bedroom. He spent the short time she was gone studying her house, approving of what he saw. It was small and looked to be a marvel of efficiency with a place for everything and everything in its place. But he would expect that from an accountant.

Lori returned in only a minute, and he grinned when he saw what was in her hand. "*Another Sea,*" she said. "Guard it like the crown jewels."

"Guaranteed. Thanks." He pocketed the book.

"You know, I have a lot of books. You might

want to go through them to see if you find something you haven't read.''

''Thank you. That would be great.''

She indicated the door to her bedroom. ''There are two closets in there. The one to the left of the dresser holds my books. Help yourself.''

Cody moved to the bedroom. Lori's big bed was covered with a thick floral comforter. In one corner of the room was a white wicker rocker, and on her long dresser stood a Tiffany lamp, a padded jewelry box and a brass tray holding an array of cosmetics. A set of four framed botanical prints had been arranged on the wall over the dresser. The room was sweetly fragrant from sachet or something. Lori was obviously a flower person. He made a mental note of the fact.

Opening the closet door, he found a science fiction treasure trove. Her collection was far more extensive than his. After scanning it, he chose two books by an author he'd never heard of and carried them out into the living room.

''Find something?'' Lori asked.

He showed her the books. ''This guy any good?''

''I don't keep anything that isn't good.'' She took a quick look. ''Oh, he's wonderful! I think that's all he's written so far.'' She tapped one of the books. "*The Sulange Warriors.* No one thinks of sci-fi as being particularly sexy, but wait until you read this one. The love scenes are terrific. The hero is stranded on a planet populated by people who have long slender tails that they can crack like whips. They use them for self-defense, but when the heroine wraps hers around the hero's waist…" Noticing the look on Cody's face, Lori stopped, feeling her face grow warm. "Well, it's not easy to explain. You'll just have to read it."

Amusement flickered in his eyes. "Sounds interesting. I can't wait."

"I really had a nice time, Cody," she said, clearing her throat. "Thanks for the wonderful meal."

"My pleasure. I'll phone tomorrow with plans."

Dipping his head, Cody gently covered her lips with his, holding the kiss for a few brief seconds. Lifting his head, he said, "See you tomorrow."

"Yes. Good night." She closed and locked the door behind him. Then she pressed her forehead to it and shut her eyes. Cody's face came into view. No wonder he was considered such a catch. He had "it"—whatever "it" was. Sex appeal, she guessed. The thing that made a woman want to make an impression.

And instinct told Lori that an infatuation with Cody Hendricks would be as disastrous to her well-being as falling in love with Michael Porter had been. He had been widowed for…what? Ten or twelve years? If he hadn't remarried in all that time, chances were good he never would. By now he probably had fashioned a wonderfully masculine world for himself with no place for a woman on any kind of permanent basis. He was ambitious, so Crystal Creek wouldn't satisfy him long. She could think of any number of reasons to be cautious where he was concerned.

Still, a tingle of excitement swept through her as she thought of tomorrow night, something she found impossible to stifle.

CODY WAS still whistling as he drove into his garage. He couldn't remember when he'd last enjoyed an evening so much. As he unlocked the door to his house, his thoughts turned to what Lori had told him about Mary Alice. He was probably clutching at straws, but… Would a woman in love for the first time do *anything* for her lover, even steal money if he asked her to? And were there really men who were that unscrupulous? He wished he knew more about Luke Harte.

Then he thought about Mary Gibson. Maybe Mary would give him a clearer picture of the kind of man Lori's friend had gotten herself mixed up with. What he could do with any new knowledge he didn't know, but he had to keep after this thing.

LORI WOKE the next morning thinking not of Cody, who had occupied her thoughts until she'd fallen asleep, but about Mary Alice. Normally she stayed out of other people's business and expected them to return the favor. Yet her feelings about Luke Harte were so strong she had to follow up on them. After working a couple of hours on her accounts, she drove to the Double C Ranch for the express purpose of doing some meddling. It was possible J.T. would have some valuable information she could use.

And she wanted to see Cynthia, too. Surprisingly, it was the mistress of the manor who answered the door. "Should you be on your feet?" Lori asked, eyeing her friend's enormous belly.

"Oh, I've been so full of energy the past couple of days," Cynthia said. "I just can't sit still. By the way, I love your hair."

"Thanks. Does it really make that much difference? Everyone I see mentions it."

"It makes a difference, believe me. Come upstairs, Lori. I want to show you the nursery now that it's finished."

The nursery, Lori decided, looked like something a film star's baby would have—color coordinated down to the talcum cans. "Cynthia, this is the prettiest nursery I've ever seen!"

"Isn't it something, and I bought almost nothing." She patted her tummy. "You wouldn't believe the gifts this child has received."

"Are you getting excited?"

"Percolating. J.T.'s even worse. And he's the one who said he was too old to have a baby. Now every other sentence starts with 'when the baby gets here.'" Cynthia beamed her pleasure.

"How is J.T. doing?" Lori asked.

"He's doing fine, but I might add that he wouldn't be doing fine if I didn't watch him and his diet like a hawk. Lord, how that man hates being told what to do! But I'll tell you, Lori—that heart attack scared the living daylights out of me. Dr. Purdy says it might have been the best thing that ever happened to him. It reminded him he isn't immortal. It also reminded him of how much he wants to be around to see this baby grow up."

"Will I disturb him too much if I ask him for a minute or two?"

"Of course not. He'll be in his study. By the way, I'm glad you stopped by. I would have been calling you later if you hadn't. Because of Thanksgiving, all of J.T.'s kids will be in one spot at the same time for the first time in ages, so we're having a little get-together Friday night. We want to invite Carolyn, Vernon and you to join us.''

"Good grief, Cynthia, isn't that a little ambitious for you at this stage of the game?''

"I feel great, and Dr. Purdy thinks I'm a week away from delivery at least. And I don't intend doing a thing Friday night. Virginia and Lettie Mae have already served notice that they're in charge, and for once I don't feel like arguing with them.''

"I'd love to come, Cynthia, I really would. Thanks.''

"And please feel free to bring a date, if you'd like.''

"Well, I...'' Lori wondered if Cody would be interested in that sort of thing...and if she had any business asking him to a family get-together after only two dates. Probably not. "I'm really not sure who I'd ask.''

Cynthia shrugged. "If you think of someone, ask him. But regardless, we want you to be here.''

"Thanks, Cynthia. Take care.''

"Oh, I will. I'm turning into a pampered princess.''

Lori left the room and went downstairs. There she encountered J.T.'s grandfather. Seeing Hank these days was always a shock to her. Of course, one could not expect a man who was on the threshold of his one-hundredth birthday to look hale and hearty, but Hank had slipped badly in the past few months.

The realization saddened Lori terribly. She sensed Hank liked her, really liked her, and that was something of an accomplishment. Not that she expected ever to hear him come right out and say so. That wouldn't have been his style at all. He worked harder at being a cantankerous, profane eccentric than anyone she had ever known. But he was wonderfully colorful, not only because of his clairvoyant powers, but also because of all those oil-patch yarns he was forever spinning. It was impossible to think of the Double C without Hank around.

"Well, good morning, Hank," she said brightly. "It's nice to see you."

"Thanks," he muttered in his gravelly voice. "I'm happy t'see you, too. 'Course, at my age I'm happy just t'*see*."

"I guess you're excited about the baby, too."

He shrugged. "Seen one baby, you've seen 'em all."

"Oh, come on. This one will be adorable, and you know it."

"Yeah, women always think babies are cute, but

I've seen a heap'a homely ones in my day. And if all babies are cute, how do you 'count for so damned many ugly grown-ups? Well, be talkin' to you.'' He adjusted his eyeglasses, then limped off, leaning heavily on his cane.

Sighing sadly, Lori turned and went down the hall that led to J.T.'s study. The door was open, and he was seated at his desk, going over some papers. She tapped lightly on the door and entered the room. J.T. looked up and smiled, getting to his feet. Lori was pleased to see him looking so fit. Someone who knew nothing of his heart attack would never have suspected he'd ever had a sick day.

''Well, hello, Lori. I almost didn't recognize you. You've done something to your hair. Come in and have a seat. What brings you over here?''

She took a chair facing his desk, and J.T. sat back down. ''I came to have a word with you, if you have a minute,'' she said.

''I have all the time you need. What can I do for you?''

''What do you know about Luke Harte?''

''I know enough not to want him working my ranch. He applied, and I turned him down.''

''Do you mind my asking why?''

''Not at all. He is lazy. Any man who works for

me has to pull his weight, and Luke doesn't. I un-
derstand he's working for Brock Munroe now.
Maybe Brock puts up with that kind of thing, but
I don't.''

''I think Brock was just desperate for an extra
pair of hands. When Luke applied for a job, did
he show you references?''

J.T. frowned in thought. ''I'm sure he did. I always ask for them.''

''Would you still have them?''

''I might, but...why on earth are you interested
in Luke, of all people?''

''Someone I think a lot of has become involved
with him, and I'd like to find out as much about
him as I can.''

J.T. seemed to accept that. Standing, he walked
to a row of filing cabinets that were lined up
against an entire wall of the study. He opened a
drawer, riffled through some folders, then grum-
bled, shut the drawer and opened another one. That
went on for some time before he found what he
was looking for. Carrying a folder to the desk, he
jerked his head toward a computer that was sitting
on a table in one corner of the room. ''All this
stuff is in that box, but I'll be damned if I can ever
get it out. I just get a lot of messages telling me
I've done something wrong. Cynthia bought the

thing and programmed it, whatever the hell that means. She says I have a closed mind, but I don't trust machines. They break down. My filing cabinets never do.'' Sitting down, he thumbed through the contents of the folder, then withdrew a sheet of paper. ''Here's Luke's application. The references are at the bottom.''

Lori took the paper and scanned it. Luke's last place of employment had been the B.J. Snyder Ranch outside Kerrville. And he had worked several places before that. He probably hadn't even listed all of them since he would have to know that no employer wanted a worker who couldn't stay in one place long. There certainly was nothing in his record to indicate he was a man who could save up enough money to buy his own ranch. He apparently had never been anything but a cowboy, and that was hardly a good-paying profession.

Lori glanced around the room. ''I see you have a copier. Would you mind my having a copy of this?''

''No, help yourself. I never use the thing. That's something else Cynthia insisted I have.''

She crossed the room to the machine. ''They're awfully handy, J.T. If you ever started using it, you'd wonder how you got along without it.''

''Humph,'' J.T. muttered. ''That's what Cynthia

says. I've got every goddamn thing you can imagine. A computer, a laser printer, a copier, a FAX machine, an answering machine I can't remember to turn on half the time. If I do happen to remember, I forget to check to see if there are any messages. I've also got speed dialing, but if I use it, how am I going to remember anyone's phone number? I don't use any of that stuff."

Resistance to change, Lori thought with a smile. The local woods were full of those types, usually men—those who wanted to do things the way they'd been done for twenty years. Changes just naturally came slowly to places like Crystal Creek, but if it were up to J.T. and his kind, they wouldn't come at all. She made her copy, then gave the original back to J.T. "I really appreciate this."

"Don't mention it."

"I'll see you soon."

"Don't stay away so long, Lori. We don't see nearly enough of you, and, hell, we're practically kinfolks."

"Maybe I'll see you Friday night. I've been invited."

"Good." J. T. stood up. "I'll see you to the door. I haven't checked up on my wife in…oh, half an hour or so."

"Are you getting excited about the baby?"

"Yeah, I am. I really am." His grin was foolish and doting.

WHEN LORI RETURNED home she immediately began making phone calls. She wasn't sure what she hoped to accomplish or why she had to pursue any secrets in Luke's past, but she couldn't shake her gut feeling that the man was leading Mary Alice straight to heartbreak.

The first number was a ranch in Colorado, but no one answered. The next was in New Mexico. The woman who answered there said the ranch's owner had recently passed away, but she would get his daughter on the phone. However, once the daughter, who introduced herself as Peggy, heard what Lori wanted, she said, "Luke? Don't mention that man's name to me! I refuse to admit that such a person ever existed!" And she hung up.

I'll bet that's a whale of a story, Lori thought, reaching to dial another number.

She fared a little better with the ranch outside Amarillo. Posing as a ranch owner, she said she was considering hiring one Luke Harte who had given this number as a reference and asked the man on the phone if he remembered Luke.

"Yeah, I remember him," he said. "A drifter with itchy feet. I can spot 'em a mile away. Usually don't have nothin' to do with 'em, but I was short-handed at the time and a little desperate. Can't say I was sorry to see him go. Some gal about…oh, I reckon she was about forty—a widow, she said—showed up three days after he left, wantin' to see him. I told her he was gone, and she asked if his mother'd had that operation. Said she'd given him some money to pay for it, said she felt sorry for the poor boy 'cause he was so worried about his mama and all. When are them women gonna learn about givin' money to drifters?''

Lori called two more numbers and heard basically the same story from them. Luke never stayed around long, and there always seemed to be some lonely woman willing to give him money in return for company and a sympathetic ear. And his mother was perpetually in need of an operation.

But it wasn't until she reached the Snyder Ranch that she found someone who was dying to talk about Luke. ''Harte?'' B.J. Snyder bellowed. ''You're damned right I remember him. Sorriest son'abitch I ever got tied up with. Funny thing, too. He *seemed* like such a nice guy. Now I've been around some time, and I like to think I can measure up a man without too much trouble, but that'un had me fooled. I even gave him some money a time or two, and I ain't a loose man with a buck. But at least I could afford what I gave him. The Davis sisters…now they're another story.''

"Davis sisters?'' By now Lori was fascinated by the story of Luke Harte, who apparently had not one redeeming virtue.

"Widowed sisters who live together in town. Luke buttered them up good, was always running errands for them, doing repairs around their house, that kinda thing. They thought he was such a 'dear boy.' Then he gave 'em some cock-and-bull story about his poor ol' mama needing an operation. Hell, he made off with practically their life savings. But lemme tell you what an oily one he is. The sisters still think he's gonna show up and repay the 'loan.' Don't that slay you? Who'd you say you are and where you're calling from? Damn, I'd like to find Harte.''

"Thank you, Mr. Snyder, but I have another call coming in and am going to have to hang up.''

"I'd like to find the son'abitch and hang him up by…''

Lori replaced the receiver in its cradle. Poor Mary Alice, she thought. But what had Lori actually accomplished? If she told Mary Alice about Luke, she would never believe her, and their friendship would be over. So all Lori'd done was find out what a complete louse Luke was, and there wasn't a thing she could do about that.

Heaving a sigh of disgust, she got up to fix herself a sandwich for lunch. After eating, she returned to her desk. She'd been working a couple of hours when Cody's call came. "Lori Porter," she answered.

"Lori, Cody."

The sound of his throaty baritone alone had the power to send a warm glow through her. "Yes, Cody."

"Cocktails at seven, dinner at eight, dancing afterwards. Is that all right with you?"

"It's fine."

"And it's black tie."

Lori tried to remember the last time she'd been to a black-tie affair and what she'd worn. What had everyone else worn? Men had it so easy when it came to this sort of thing. "It sounds very festive," she said calmly, as though such events were old hat to her.

"Good. I'll see you tonight at, say, six-thirty."

"Fine. I'll be ready."

After hanging up, Lori stared at the papers on her desk for a minute, then stood up and went to her closet in the bedroom. She fingered virtually every garment hanging there, but nothing looked just right. Fleetingly she considered trying to borrow something from Beverly, but thought better of it. Beverly could stop traffic when she got dressed to the nines, but compared to Lori she was a bit on the flashy side. Beverly could get away with it beautifully, but Lori knew the really wild stuff would only look silly on her.

On an impulse, she returned to her desk, grabbed the phone and dialed. Her call was answered on the fourth ring.

"Hello."

"Amanda, thank God I found you. This is Lori."

"Hi, Lori. What's up?"

"I need help. I have a major date tonight, black tie, and you're going to have to dress me."

"Do you care if you have to spend something?"

"Within reason, no."

"I'm on the way," Amanda said without hesitation.

Breathing a sigh of relief, Lori hung up. Amanda wouldn't steer her wrong.

CHAPTER SIX

IT WAS LATE AFTERNOON, and the day's work was done. Luke Harte lay on his bunk in the Double Bar's bunkhouse, resting. He was awash in contentment and savoring every second of it. After a lot of lousy years, things were going his way at last. He had an undemanding job, his favorite kind. He had some money in the bank, and a girlfriend who was the answer to a man's prayer. Mary Alice was sweet, receptive and adoring. Maybe a little short in the looks department, but he could live with that.

He glanced at the clock on the wall, then reached in the drawer of the table beside his bunk and withdrew a small black book. It was a passbook issued to him by a bank in Fredericksburg. Opening it, he smiled as he looked at the neat columns of figures. It was the most satisfying thing in the world to know he could walk into that bank, shove the passbook toward a teller and get as much of that sum as he wanted. No one would ever know how long it had taken him to put so much money together.

Since the day he'd left Rawlins, Wyoming, that was how long—ten years ago when he was nineteen. He would have left long before that, but he hadn't had the money. It seemed his whole damned life had been one long search for money.

He sometimes thought of Rawlins. Not often and not for very long and not with any fond memories, but he guessed he'd never forget it entirely. He'd had to work in his dad's hardware store after school and on Saturdays for as long as he could remember, and his old man had been impossible to please. But that had been preferable to staying at home with his sad-faced mother. If she'd ever once been happy, Luke didn't know anything about it. Of course, he didn't see how anyone could be happy living with his father, who was as demanding of his wife as he was of his son. The man had reserved his approval strictly for Luke's lazy, spoiled sister. Luke supposed he should occasionally wonder about his family, how they were doing, but he never did.

In those days his hunger to enrich himself had been like a festering wound. By his mid-teens he had figured out there were two kinds of people in the world—those who had ''Yes, sir'' said to them a dozen times a day and those who had to do the saying. He had wanted to be called "sir" so badly it was something he could taste, and he'd known he never would be in Rawlins, so he had lit out.

The names of towns he had been in since ran through his mind—Greeley, Santa Rosa, Amarillo, Lubbock, Midland, down to San Angelo before he headed to Kerrville. Of all the ranches he had worked, this one, the Double Bar, was the smallest. But to date, Brock Munroe had treated him okay and wasn't demanding or nosy. Shoot, he and his pretty squeeze, Amanda, were so wrapped up in each other and that big ol' house, Luke figured he could get away with just about anything.

Soon after leaving Wyoming, he had discovered that being a cowboy meant a lot of work for very little pay, but about that time he also had discovered his attractiveness to women. He had used it to full advantage ever since. No one would ever get rich working cows, but there were so many lonely women out there who would do anything for a kind word and a smile. His gift of gab and his smile had done more for him than his strong back ever had.

He'd once thought about getting married—to

the daughter of the man he'd worked for in New Mexico. Her old man had seemed to Luke to be rich as Midas with all that land and all those cattle. The woman, Peg, had been a trifle on the homely side, but that hardly mattered if she had money.

Unfortunately, from one of Peg's brothers-in-law he'd learned that the rancher had sewed up the money so tightly that no in-law could ever lay claim to more than had been arranged for in the prenuptial agreement. That was the first time Luke had learned there were people who actually sat down before a wedding and decided who got what if there was a divorce.

The brother-in-law further informed him that the in-law's share wasn't a hell of a lot. After that, Peg's homeliness seemed to intensify, and Luke hadn't stayed long. He'd decided marriage wasn't necessary to get what he hungered for.

He glanced once more at the passbook, as if reassuring himself that it actually was his. Then he placed it back in the drawer, rolled off the bunk and stood up, heading for the shower at the end of the room. The sweeter he smelled, the sweeter Mary Alice was to him. And she could be very sweet indeed. He sometimes thought the word *sweet* had been coined to describe the Mary Alices of the world—the shy little creatures who wanted to fade into the woodwork and never offend anyone.

After showering and shaving, he dressed in pressed jeans, a starched white shirt and his best boots. He combed his hair, trimmed his mustache and splashed on after-shave. Stepping back, he admired himself in the mirror before grabbing a jacket and his new Stetson and heading for the pickup parked outside.

The truck was a disgrace, but he wasn't about to spend precious dollars for another one as long as this one ran. He almost had a fit every time the damned ol' thing needed a new part or tires. He couldn't believe what things cost these days. The engine sputtered twice, died, then turned over on the third try. Luke drove out of the ranch's main gate and headed for Crystal Creek. Mary Alice and her mother lived on the west side of town in a small three-bedroom that desperately needed paint, some yard work and general fixing up. He knew he could further endear himself to the two women by coming over and playing handyman, but so far he hadn't worked up the energy to do so. Really hard work was not what he did best, not unless the rewards were worth it.

Mary Alice answered the door. He had to give

her credit for one thing—she always looked band-box fresh, even in jeans. An adoring smile wreathed her face. "Hi," she said in that timid way of hers.

"Hi. I'm not late, am I?"

"No, you're right on time. Come in."

He stepped into the living room. It was a homey, old-fashioned room, furnished with odds and ends, most of them well-worn. It reminded him of the one in Rawlins.

"We're having pot roast tonight," Mary Alice said. "I hope you like it."

Of course she did. She hoped he liked everything. She hoped *everybody* liked everything. That was what Luke found hardest to accept about Mary Alice—that pathetic eagerness to please. Sometimes he wanted to tell her to stop apologizing her way through life, to display a little backbone and grit. But then he would remind himself that a Mary Alice with backbone and grit would not be the sweet, willing, agreeable woman she was.

"Pot roast? I love it," he assured her. "Can't say I've gotten a bad meal in this house yet."

Mary Alice took him by the hand. "Come on, say hello to Mom."

Norma Priest was in the kitchen, seated on a

stool at the counter, peeling potatoes. She was a tall, thin woman in her late forties. Life had not been gentle with her, and her expression reflected that. Her back trouble was the latest in a long list of nuisance ailments that had plagued her since Mary Alice's birth. Her husband had left her for another woman when Mary Alice was three, and their existence had been at the subsistence level ever since. She was by trade a hairdresser, but she had changed to manicurist when her bad back had made long hours on her feet torturous. Without Mary Alice's job, she didn't know what they would have done.

Luke Harte, Norma had decided, was a savior. When her daughter had first brought him to the house, she had been maternally suspicious. The young cowboy was one of the best-looking men she had ever seen, and though she adored Mary Alice, Norma knew her daughter was no beauty. She had envisioned all sorts of ulterior motives for Luke's interest in the girl.

But several months had passed, and she now had decided Luke was genuinely smitten, that he saw beneath the rather plain exterior to the lovely woman inside. Now Norma prayed nightly that he would marry Mary Alice, buy the ranch he talked about and allow her to live with them, as he'd promised. To never again have to go to the shop when her back was killing her sounded like paradise. It was almost all she could think about. When her daughter and the cowboy entered the kitchen, Norma's face broke into a rare and radiant smile.

"Evenin', Mrs. Priest," Luke greeted her. "Something sure smells good."

"Hope it tastes like it smells then," Norma said. "And I've told you three dozen times you can call me Norma."

"No, ma'am. My mama, well, she'd think I was being downright disrespectful. She used to tell me it was rude to call people older'n you by their first name." The lie tripped lightly off Luke's tongue. His mother hadn't given him five minutes' worth of advice in his life that he could recall.

"Sit down, Luke. Mary Alice, get the boy something to drink."

"A beer all right, Luke?" Mary Alice asked.

"That'll be fine."

Mary Alice went to the refrigerator, took out a can, popped the top and brought it to him. Then she sat down at the table, clasped her hands in front of her and fastened that wide-eyed, enraptured expression on him. "What kind of day did you have?" she asked, as she invariably did.

"Same as always. Slavery, pure and simple."

"I wish you didn't have to work so hard," Mary Alice said sympathetically.

"It wouldn't be so bad if I was working for myself. Just don't like breaking my back for someone else."

Mary Alice smiled, and within seconds Luke had slipped into his favorite role—charming, desirable man. The two women hung on his every word. How he loved it! For some men it was a studied, practiced pose, learned and perfected by trial and error over the years. Some men never learned to play the part. For Luke Harte, it was as effortless and natural as breathing.

BY THE TIME six-thirty rolled around that evening, Lori had put Mary Alice's involvement with Luke at the bottom of her worry list and was instead bubbling with excitement over tonight's date with Cody. She found herself doing the silliest things—rearranging throw pillows, straightening lampshades and checking her appearance in the mirror for the umpteenth time.

Amanda had insisted she wear simple black with gold jewelry, and though it hadn't sounded exciting at the time, now Lori admitted her friend knew what she was talking about. The clothes and jewelry both were expensive, and with her hair wound into a French twist, she looked…well, sophisticated. When the doorbell rang, again at precisely the appointed hour, she jumped, then ran to answer it. Cody stood on the front stoop, his peerless smile wreathing his face. Lori hoped her own smile didn't look as ridiculous as it felt.

"Hi," he said, then let out a soft whistle. "Lori, you look absolutely stunning."

Cody Hendricks in black tie was a feast for feminine eyes, she decided. "Thank you. Please come in. Has it gotten much colder?"

"It's just brisk." He handed her something. "Before I forget—here it is, safe and sound. Thanks for letting me read it."

Lori took the book and laid it on a nearby table. "You're welcome. Did you like it?"

"Very much. You were right. The genius was there even then."

She reached for a beaded black stole, which he placed over her shoulders. Opening the door, he stepped aside. "Do you leave that light on?" he asked, indicating a small lamp beside an easy chair.

"Yes, I hate coming home to a dark house."

"So do I." He closed the door behind them, and Lori locked it.

"Do you have an apartment or a house, Cody?" she asked as they walked to his car.

"I rent a house. Ridiculous waste of money, but I couldn't find anything I wanted to buy." He opened the passenger door, and she slid in. "Maybe I'll build one of these days."

After he had slid behind the wheel and turned on the engine, Lori asked, "In Crystal Creek?"

Unlikely, he thought. "I guess so...if I stay here."

"How would you feel about settling down here?"

He shrugged. "The place has been good to me so far, and I'd be lying if I said I didn't like being in charge."

"Would you also be lying if you said you wouldn't like being in charge of a bigger branch?"

He grinned. "Yeah, I would."

"Maybe even CEO someday?"

Cody tensed, then realized she was only making idle conversation. "Lori, if that ever happens, which it won't, I'll be a very, very old man." Shifting into gear, he turned the car around and headed for the gate. "Did you get a lot of work done today?"

"Not really. But I did discover that my instincts are in good working order. Luke Harte is a rat."

"Oh?"

Succinctly she told him about her phone calls. Cody listened with what appeared to be casual interest, but he hung on every word. "Wow!" he exclaimed when she finished. "It might be interesting to follow that guy around for a few days, just to watch him operate."

Lori shot him an admonishing look. "A thoroughly masculine remark if I ever heard one."

Cody chuckled. "Well, you have to admit he must have something us ordinary men don't."

"A man like that should be put behind bars," she said with a sniff.

"A thoroughly feminine remark if I ever heard one," he said and winked at her.

"Sadly, I don't suppose there's anything at all illegal about what Luke does. Unethical maybe, but not against the law. If all those women willingly gave him money without asking a thing in return…" She shrugged. "I don't guess you really could put him behind bars."

"Not if the money was theirs to give."

Lori looked at him. "What do you mean by that?"

"Only that the guy apparently is such a smooth operator that a woman might get money for him by shady means."

"Mmm, I hadn't thought about that." Lori idly stared through the windshield. "I've never had anything but hors d'oeuvres at the country club. Is the food any good?"

"Not bad, but I bet I can tell you exactly what we'll be served tonight."

"What?"

"Salad, prime rib, baked potato and baked Alaska."

"How do you know that?"

"Because I've been to dozens of these sit-down affairs at the club, and that's what was served at every single one of them. If it were lunch, we'd have chicken. To my knowledge, that's all they know how to make."

HALF AN HOUR LATER, Cody propped himself against a wall in the bar and watched Lori as she spoke to Tom Fuentes and his wife, Millie. He had just introduced her to them, and she was charming their socks off, especially Tom, who couldn't take his eyes off her. Cody could see why. With the interest of a connoisseur, he studied the lovely woman who was his date tonight. The very simplicity of her dress made her stand out amidst the shine and glitter, beads and diamonds, like a hybrid rose in a cabbage patch.

Cody sipped his drink and watched as Lori smiled at Millie Fuentes, casually projecting an air of unstudied sophistication and unconscious sex appeal. The traits were all the more appealing because she seemed completely unaware that she possessed them.

At that moment, she said a few words of parting to Tom and Millie and turned toward him, coming to his side with a smile.

"Having a good time?" Cody asked.

"It's a lovely party," Lori said. "Very glitzy."

"That's not what I asked you."

"Of course I'm having a good time. Why wouldn't I be?"

Cody shrugged. "Oh, I don't know. These things always seem to reek with superficiality. I don't think any of these people are really having as much fun as they seem to be."

"Why, Cody Hendricks. You sound positively jaded and world-weary."

He smiled. Slipping a hand beneath her elbow,

he said, "Shall we mix and mingle or stand here and hold up this wall?"

Lori pretended to study the wall. "Oh...it looks pretty sturdy to me. I doubt we'll be necessary."

Holding her elbow in a firm grip, Cody propelled her through the crowd, stopping occasionally to introduce her to someone else. Lori knew she'd never remember half the people she'd met this evening or ever see most of them again. She hadn't encountered more than a dozen familiar faces all evening, but she had meant it when she told Cody she was having a good time. The glitz and glitter were fun for a change, and it was fun to have a reason to really dress up. But mostly she was enjoying being with her companion. Cody's party manner was perfection itself. He was witty and intelligent, suave and relaxed. He was a whiz with names; not once did he stumble.

And he knew exactly how to treat a woman. Every time she spoke to him he trained his attention on her as though he found what she was saying to be the most fascinating thing he had ever heard. Of course, she reminded herself, practice made perfect, and from what she'd heard, Cody must have had more practice with women that anyone she'd ever known. Lori didn't think she had imagined the envious glances she'd received from half the women present. Whenever she felt covetous eyes upon her, she inched in a little closer to him. And each time she did, he smiled down at her, prompting her smile in return, giving the deceptive impression to others that they were very close indeed. Yes, she had to admit it was fun...like an adult senior prom.

The evening fairly raced by. Lori couldn't believe it was well after midnight when Cody parked in front of her house. Instead of immediately getting out of the car, he turned off the engine and the headlights, then shifted in the seat to face her.

"The prime rib was good, wasn't it?" she said.

"Pretty good. Thanks for coming with me tonight."

"Thank *you* for asking me."

"You'll be going home for Thanksgiving, I suppose."

"Oh, yes. Grandma's written it on her calendar. I'd more easily change the flow of the tides than change something on Grandma's calendar."

Cody chuckled. "Are you leaving tomorrow?"

"No, I'll drive down early Thursday and back the next morning."

Reaching out, he curled a wisp of hair behind her ear. "Then how about having dinner with me tomorrow night at that German place out on the highway?''

Three nights in a row? Lori was definitely flattered, a little perplexed, completely intrigued. By accepting another date with him, which she intended doing, she would be telling him she had the world's deadest social life. But she might as well enjoy this as long as it lasted. ''I really like their food,'' she said. ''Thanks, Cody. I'd love to.''

''I'll call tomorrow.''

The hand that had been toying with her hair moved to her nape, and as he bent his head, he moved her face closer to his. Alive with anticipation, Lori knew she wasn't going to get another light brush of his lips.

She was right. His mouth covered hers in a kiss that sent sparks sputtering through her. At first it was light, coaxing, exploring, but as she responded to it, Cody deepened the kiss. While he held her nape with one hand, his other drifted slowly down her spine and came to rest at the small of her back. His mouth slowly opened and his tongue traced the seam of her lips.

Lori supposed the kiss belonged in the ''sweet'' category, so she couldn't understand the tumult of emotions it elicited. When he finally broke the kiss, she felt the pounding of her heart and was aware of the silly, breathless look on her face. She fully expected to find Cody looking at her with amusement over her reaction, but his expression clearly told her the kiss had moved him, too. A wave of pleasure flooded her, and she sat back, a bemused look of self-satisfaction on her face.

"You're a lovely lady," he said.

"Thank you."

"I like you."

"I...like you, too."

Then, in a gesture that was as startling as a slap would have been, he lifted one of her hands and studied it a second before slowly turning it over and kissing her palm...as if he was savoring the taste of her skin. No one had ever kissed her hand before. It was tormentingly gentle.

And over in a split second. Reaching behind him, Cody opened his door and got out. Rounding the car, he opened hers and gave her his hand. At her door, he pulled her close and held her against him and his good-night kiss was gentle. Once she was inside the house, she listened as he drove away, thinking that of all the men she had ever known, Cody was the only one who could probably sweep a woman off her feet.

But... There was a nagging "but." Lori was

very intuitive about people, and she sensed there
was something more to Cody Hendricks than met
the eye, part of him that was never revealed. She
couldn't imagine what it was, but there was something. She'd bet on it.

HOWEVER, Cody was so charming that by the time
he brought her home Wednesday night, Lori had
all but conceded her heart to the handsome banker
with the smile that could melt ice cubes. It had
been another wonderful evening, although nothing at all remarkable had transpired. They had
simply sat in a secluded booth in a rustic German
restaurant, eating kraut and knockwurst, drinking
beer and talking…and talking. At one point, Cody
remarked, "By the way, I was out at Mary Gibson's place today. I asked her about your 'friend,'
Luke Harte."

"Oh? What did she have to say about him?"

"She said he's a dear boy."

Lori sniffed. "Mary would think that because
she likes everybody and doesn't have a suspicious
bone in her body."

"She also said he has a tough time of it financially and had asked to borrow some money a
couple of times. Mary regretted having to turn
him down, but she simply didn't have it to lend."

"Thank heavens for that! Maybe that will save Mary Alice from being taken. I don't think she has any to lend, either."

Another tidbit clicked into place in Cody's mind.

"Are you going to Houston tomorrow?" Lori asked.

"Yes, but I'll be back tomorrow night. The bank is open for business Friday. Since you'll be back Friday, too, I was wondering if you might like to go to Zack's that night."

Somehow Zack's and Cody didn't seem to jibe. The popular honky-tonk drew a young crowd as a rule, but by now Lori realized there was a lot about Cody that didn't jibe with his public image. She had opened her mouth to accept when she remembered the dinner invitation from the McKinneys. "Well, as a matter of fact, the McKinneys have asked me to dinner that night. Seems all J.T.'s kids are going to be in one spot at the same time, so the family's having a small party. But Cynthia also told me to bring someone. I'd love to have you come with me if that sort of thing appeals to you at all."

"Wouldn't I be horning in on a family thing?"

"Not at all. It will be very casual. You know the McKinneys, don't you?"

Cody nodded. "I guess I've met all of them. I know J.T. and Tyler best, though."

"I'd really like for you to come."

"Then I accept with pleasure."

They lingered over dessert and coffee, often gazing into each other's eyes like love-struck teenagers. Cody's gaze felt like a physical caress—intimate and sensual. It was hard to believe that this time last week he had been merely a nodding acquaintance.

Lori was reluctant to have the interlude end, but end it did when they noticed the restaurant had emptied and the staff apparently were waiting for them to leave. Tomorrow night she would be in the bosom of family, usually something so comforting, but this time she feared she would spend most of the holiday thinking about Cody. It helped some to know she was going to be with him Friday night, and she marveled that she had become so attached to a man in such an incredibly short time.

At her door, he gathered her into his arms and gazed at her with such solemnity that her heart knocked against her ribs. Then he kissed her deeply, with unhurried thoroughness—once, twice, three times. Lori melted into each kiss, returning each with intensity. They had certainly come a long way from that brush of his lips against hers Monday night. At that moment, if he had asked to come in and spend the night, she would have unhesitatingly said yes.

However, he didn't. Breaking the final kiss, Cody held her a moment, then stepped back. "Have a nice Thanksgiving."

"Y-you...too."

"I'll call you Friday. Inside with you now."

He isn't an easy man to figure out, Lori thought as she got ready for bed. His reputation as a Lothario, a Don Juan, was so at odds with the man she thought she was beginning to know. Lotharios lunged at the first opportunity, didn't they? Cody seemed perfectly willing to take a relationship one step at a time—a light kiss on the first night, a sweet one on the second, then the ones tonight that were passionately restrained. She could only wonder what Friday night would bring. The mere thought sent a shiver of anticipation up and down her spine. Friday night was going to be hard to wait for.

WHEN THURSDAY MORNING dawned, Lori was glad there was something she had to do that day, something that would take her mind off tomorrow night. Rising early, she made coffee, passing up breakfast with Carolyn and Vernon because she knew how much food she would be expected to consume that day. After showering and dressing, she packed an overnight bag and headed south for San Antonio.

The house Lori had grown up in was in a northwest suburb of the city, an older, quiet neighborhood that had been well kept. The two-storied white structure was shaded by enormous trees that her father had planted when she was a small girl.

She arrived at ten o'clock Thursday morning, parked her car in the driveway and sprinted up the front steps. Punching the doorbell twice to herald her arrival, she pushed open the door and stepped inside. The smells of Thanksgiving assailed her nostrils—sage dressing, pumpkin pie, yeast rolls and, of course, roasting turkey.

"I'm here!" she called.

Her mother, Marian DeMarco, came down the stairs. She was an attractive woman in her early sixties, trim and well-groomed. "Hello, darling. What have you done to your hair?"

"I got a perm. Like it?"

"Love it. Yes, it's very becoming. Was the traffic bad?"

The two women embraced at the foot of the

stairs. "Very light. I guess almost everyone traveled yesterday. Where's Grandma?"

"Where do you think? In the kitchen, where she's been for the past three days."

"What does she *do* in there?" Lori asked. "I could understand these marathons in the kitchen when everyone still lived at home, but now... Is anyone else coming?"

"Just Francis and Henrietta, and Anna has fixed enough food for a convention. Be prepared to take a lot home with you."

Mother and daughter fell in step and crossed the big dining room, heading for the kitchen. "How's Carolyn?" Marian asked.

"She's fine and sends her love."

"What's her new husband like?"

"A prince."

In the big kitchen, Anna DeMarco stood at her favorite spot, in front of the stove. On the table in the center of the room were four pies and two cakes. She had baked four pies and two cakes every Thanksgiving of her adult life, and it wouldn't have occurred to her to do otherwise simply because there was no one to eat so much food.

She was an amazing woman. Married at seventeen, she had spent the majority of the next sixty-odd years in a kitchen. She honestly believed that if a woman wasn't feeding her family, getting ready to feed her family or just finishing feeding her family, she really wasn't doing much of anything.

"Hello, Grandma," Lori said, coming up to slip her arms around Anna's ample waist. "Everything smells wonderful."

Anna paused to pat her granddaughter's hand. "Lori, darling. What on earth have you done to your hair?"

"Like it?"

"I'm not sure. It's not…you. I hope you're hungry."

Lori surveyed the contents of all the pots and pans. Two kinds of potatoes, three vegetables. All for five people. It was almost obscene. "Everything looks wonderful, Grandma. I'll try to do it justice."

Anna put down her spoon and turned to give her granddaughter her full attention. "Have you lost weight?"

"Not an ounce."

"You look thin and tired. Doesn't she look thin and tired, Marian?"

Marian scrutinized Lori. "She looks fine to me."

"I'm neither thin nor tired," Lori vowed. "I feel wonderful."

"Come over here. Let's sit down." The two women sat at the dessert-laden table. "I worry about you," Anna said.

"I know you do, Grandma, but you shouldn't."

"What do you eat?"

Marian shook her head, rolled her eyes and left the room. Lori chuckled. "What do I eat? I eat...all kinds of things."

"What did you have to eat yesterday?"

"Oh, Lord, I don't remember. Let's see... Well, I had a chicken pot pie for lunch."

"Frozen?" Anna's tone was disapproving.

"Of course frozen! I *work,* Grandma. I don't have time to stew a chicken and make piecrust and..."

Lori stopped and uttered a little sigh. She'd never understood her grandmother's preoccupation with food, only that it was as much a part of Anna DeMarco as her decisive dark eyes. "I'll tell you down to the last detail what I had for dinner Monday night, though. Pounds of barbecue! My date took me to Cooper's in Llano, and we had..."

Now Lori had hit on something that interested Anna even more than food. "You had a date?"

"Why do you make that sound like the most incredible thing you've ever heard? Of course I had a date. I've had lots of dates."

"What's his name? What's he like? What does he do?"

"His name is Cody Hendricks, and he is a very nice man."

Anna frowned. "Cody. Is he a cowboy? That sounds like a cowboy's name."

"No, he isn't a cowboy. Far from it. He's a vice president with Southwest Bank, and he manages the Crystal Creek branch. I'm sure some day he'll be a very big shot with Southwest. He's the type."

The look on her grandmother's face caused Lori to choke back a laugh. Instant approval. "Oh, Lori, that's wonderful! You do like him, I hope."

"Yes, I like him very much. We went out Tuesday night and last night, and we're going to have dinner with the McKinneys tomorrow night." *That* ought to give her grandmother food for thought.

"How splendid! You work hard at this, Lori. Someone like a banker...well, he'll always be there for you."

Lori couldn't help it. This time she had to

laugh. "You don't know the first thing about him."

"I know about such things, darling. Believe me, I do. You don't have to know a man forever to know he's the one for you. The first time I met your grandfather I knew he was the man I was going to marry."

"Of course you did. Your parents arranged the marriage when you both were twelve."

"Parents were smarter in those days." Anna sniffed, then stood up and went to the oven to baste the turkey.

NATURALLY, the meal was something to write a poem about. The menu had never varied through all the years Lori could remember, but this Thanksgiving dinner would stand out in memory for one reason: Henrietta, Uncle Francis's fiancée.

She was the most overwhelmingly vivacious person Lori had ever met. Her appeal wasn't exclusively the mass of red hair or the ample bosom that shook when she laughed. It was the *joie de vivre* she exuded. She talked, she laughed, she gestured, and she completely dominated the conversation throughout the meal.

From time to time Lori's gaze wandered to Francis. Never a talkative person, today he had scarcely uttered a word. Her uncle's pale gray eyes were riveted on his fiancée, and the look on his face was one of absolute adoration. Lori could certainly understand his fascination with Henrietta, but why on earth would such a woman be interested in a colorless character like him?

But perhaps that was the very attraction. Henrietta got no competition from Francis, only adoration and approval, leaving her to be the star of the show. And as Lori and Marian were cleaning the kitchen after the gigantic meal, Lori suddenly thought of Mary Alice and Luke. Maybe that was the attraction there, too. Strutting, swaggering Luke with shy, adoring Mary Alice. *Maybe I should stop worrying about Mary Alice so and start being happy that she's at least having an experience.* Even an experience that led to heartbreak, Lori decided, was better than no experience at all. Perhaps that was the reason she was rushing headlong toward an infatuation with Cody.

An involuntary sigh escaped her lips. Marian turned to her with a frown. "Something wrong, Lori?"

"No, Mom. Nothing's wrong. It's been a wonderful Thanksgiving, as usual."

Marian studied her daughter for a moment.

"You know, darling, you've lost something these past few years."

Lori looked at her with a start. "You mean like a husband?"

"No, something else. Zest, gaiety, *life.* It's almost as though you're existing but not really living."

"I'm…hoping that's changing." Lori returned her attention to the dishes she was scraping.

"There's someone?"

"You sound just like Grandma."

"Maybe. But unlike Anna, I don't insist on marriage. I'm thinking it wouldn't hurt you to do something a little rash and impulsive once in a while. Something more exciting than simply getting a new hairdo."

"For instance?"

Marian laughed. "I don't know. Take a cruise, fall in love, have an affair. Let the devil take tomorrow. Something."

"That's really not very sound motherly advice."

"Maybe not, but it's sound woman-to-woman advice, believe me."

Marian said it with such conviction that Lori wondered if her mother had done anything rash and impulsive since her father's death. Fallen in love, had an affair? It was an absolutely stunning thought.

AT THAT MOMENT, in the River Oaks mansion where Cody had grown up, the Hendricks clan was gathering in the library for an after-dinner brandy. The men and women present—a smattering of aunts and uncles and cousins had joined the family for Thanksgiving—all were faultlessly and expensively dressed. Informality was seldom employed in the household. DeWitt, particularly, was one of those men whose clothes never seemed to lose their crease or get rumpled. Cody watched as his father walked to the fireplace, propped one foot on the hearth and gazed over the assemblage. That simple act had the immediate effect of training all eyes on him, something Cody suspected it was meant to do.

Everyone in the room was, to some extent, married to Southwest Bank, so these after-dinner gatherings usually were more like business meetings than anything. This afternoon was no exception. The only difference was that today DeWitt seemed uncommonly interested in the tiny Crystal Creek branch.

"It's come to my attention that you authorize a great many farm and ranch loans," he said to

Cody. "Do you think that's wise? It's not a very stable business."

"Farming and ranching are Crystal Creek's lifeblood, Dad. I agree it's a feast-or-famine enterprise, but rural people are the last word in stability. They've set down roots, so they don't cut and run when things get rough. They stay and work them out. I haven't had a foreclosure yet."

"The ostrich farm was pretty hard to swallow," DeWitt added. "I certainly hope you investigated the viability of such an operation."

"Of course I did. Mary will make a go of it, I'm sure of that. You see, Dad, I lent the money to a person, not an operation." It irritated Cody no end that his judgment was being questioned in front of the entire family, though he knew he should have become accustomed to it by now.

As usual, his arguments fell on unsympathetic ears. DeWitt changed the subject. "There's a special meeting of the board of directors Tuesday morning. Be here. And Luther Thorpe's retirement party is Thursday night. I wouldn't want you to miss it."

That was not the way Cody had planned to spend the coming week, but he hardly could refuse. In fact, he didn't want to refuse. He was a member of the board, and he truly liked Luther

Thorpe. But he bristled at being ordered to attend. Beyond the family circle, he was treated like an intelligent adult who was perfectly capable of making decisions. He had only to come home to be treated like a child.

He left as soon as he decently could. As usual, driving away from the formidable mansion was like shedding a burden. He had grown up in a world where enough green stuff could turn anybody's blood blue. It was an endless status game of mansions, cars, clothes, jewels, parties and "good works." No wonder, Cody reflected, he enjoyed Crystal Creek so much. As he drove past the sign announcing the town limits, he experienced a profound sense of homecoming. The only thing that would have made him feel even better was if Lori was home. After being with his family, he could use a heavy dose of her.

CHAPTER SEVEN

MARY ALICE THUMBED through the television listings and pulled a face. Putting down the guide,
she picked up a paperback novel. Yesterday had
been wonderful. Luke had eaten Thanksgiving
dinner with them and stayed at the house all day.
Now it was Friday night, the worst night of the
week, the one when she had no hope of seeing
Luke. Brock needed him, he'd told her, and Mary
Alice thought it grossly unfair of his boss to make
an employee work *every* Friday night.

Her mother came out of the kitchen. "No
TV?" she asked.

"There's nothing on."

"There must be something," Norma insisted,
crossing the room and turning on the set.

"You just like the noise," Mary Alice com-
plained.

"Guess I do," Norma agreed, settling herself
in her favorite chair and focusing on the screen.

Mary Alice tried to concentrate on the book,

but after a few minutes she gave up and went into her bedroom.

The room still looked much as it had when she was in high school, except now it was shabbier. She had bought a new bedspread at a discount store sale last year, but she didn't like it all that much. She hated the whole room. Green and yellow hadn't been fashionable for years and years. She had told Luke she wanted a blue-and-mauve bedroom when they got married, and he'd told her he'd make damned sure she got one. Mary Alice thought mauve was about the classiest color there was.

She plopped on the bed, folded her arms behind her head and stared at the ceiling, smiling. He had been so sweet and loving the night before. She had finally asked him where he intended buying the ranch, and he'd told her he was looking at a place near Fort Worth. Funny, she hadn't even once thought they would have to move so far away, but since her mother would be with them, she didn't suppose it mattered where they lived.

Turning her head, she glanced at the bedside clock. Lord, it wasn't even seven yet, and she was so bored and restless she wanted to jump out of her skin. Maybe moving away wouldn't be so bad after all. There had been a time—about a hundred years ago it seemed—when the thought of leaving Crystal Creek would have devastated her, but that was when she was in high school. She'd never run with an "in" crowd or anything close to it, but she'd had some friends. Now the few who still lived in town were married and had babies, so there was no one to hang out with. It was the same with her co-workers at the bank. Only Debbie Watson was near her own age, and Mary Alice frankly thought Debbie was a snob who considered herself better than the Priests.

Just then the phone rang, and she bolted upright, reaching for it. "I'll get it!" she yelled as she picked up the receiver. "Hello."

"Hi, sugar."

"Oh, Luke." A delicious thought came to mind. Maybe he was getting the night off after all. "Where are you?"

"I'm at the bunkhouse, but I'm fixin' to leave."

"Leave?"

"Yeah, Brock's got about a hundred things for me to do tonight."

"On Friday night?"

"Kills you, right? Wonder what he did before I came along. He works me like a slave."

"Oh," Mary Alice said with a pout. "I was

hoping you were calling to say you'd be coming by."

"'Fraid not. I just wanted to check up on you and give you my love."

"That's sweet."

"Listen, sugar…you know all that stuff I told you about that ranch that's for sale? I'd rather you didn't mention that to anyone. Don't even tell your mama."

Mary Alice frowned. "Why?"

"'Cause there's way too much gossipin' goin' on at that beauty shop, for one thing, and as much as I love your mama to death, she does like to chat. And for another, I'd just as soon Brock didn't get wind of the fact I don't intend workin' for him the rest of my life. He might fire me, and I'm not quite ready to quit yet."

"I…I guess I can understand that."

"And the place promises to be a steal. The old boy who owns it wants to go live with his daughter in California, and he's anxious. Someone might hear about it and grab it out from under me."

"Okay, Luke, I won't say a word." It occurred to her that she might already have said too much to Lori, but how could she have known? If Luke felt that way, he should have told her earlier.

"Another thing. When it comes time, I'm gonna want you to leave on a minute's notice. Can you do that?"

"Oh, Luke...I have to give notice at the bank. I couldn't do that to them. And Mama wouldn't want to go off and leave the shop without a manicurist."

Mary Alice heard a sound of impatience on the other end of the line. "Aw, you two aren't gonna need the bank and the beauty shop once we leave here. What are they gonna do—arrest you for quitting without notice?"

"Well, no, but..."

"It'll be a clean break for both of you."

"It sounds so exciting."

"I'm hoping it will be, sugar. Yes, indeed, I'm hoping it's gonna be very exciting. Well...guess I'd better get a move on. I'll see you tomorrow afternoon."

"Okay, Luke. I love you."

"And I love you, too, sugar."

"Good night, Luke."

Mary Alice hung up, folded her hands in her lap and sighed heavily. It promised to be a long night, but knowing they would spend most of tomorrow together was somewhat consoling. She thought back over last year and the year before that—actually all the years since high school. They had been lonely and uneventful, but her mother had cautioned her not to expect life to be exciting. So the best Mary Alice had ever dreamed of was that something interesting would happen to her someday.

Now there was Luke, who was both interesting and exciting. He was all she could think about anymore. She even found it hard to concentrate at work, but as Luke had said, the job wasn't as important to her as it once had been. She had so much more to think about now than growing to be an old maid behind a teller's cage at Southwest Bank.

Mary Alice felt somehow blessed, and she wondered what on earth she had done with her time before Luke had come into her life.

THE MINUTE Luke hung up the phone he went in to take a shower. When he came out, he put on fresh jeans, a denim shirt and his work boots. After slipping on his jacket, he reached in the drawer beside his bunk and withdrew a gift-wrapped package. Frowning, he considered it a minute. He wished he could have come up with something a little more original than cologne, but the lady at the drugstore had said the fragrance was all the rage. "Whoever receives that will be impressed," she'd promised. "Trust me."

She ought'a be, he thought. *Fifty lousy bucks.* He put the package in his pocket, gave his appearance another glance in the mirror, then left the bunkhouse, climbed in the pickup and headed for Crystal Creek, just as he had every Friday night for three months.

"DID YOU HAVE a nice Thanksgiving?" Cody asked as he helped Lori on with her coat.

"Wonderful. Pounds of food. Grandma cooked for three days." She turned to face him. "I guess it was the same at your house."

He checked a smile. He doubted if his mother even knew where the kitchen was. "There was a lot of food."

"There'll be a lot tonight, too. Lettie Mae, the McKinneys' cook, is a kitchen genius."

"I did get some bad news while I was home, though."

Lori's eyes widened. "Oh, Cody, I'm so sorry!"

But he smiled. "It's just that I'm going to have to be gone next week. A meeting of the great minds has been called," he said, carefully avoiding any reference to the board of directors, "and a friend is having a retirement party."

"That *is* dreadful news," she teased.

"We'll have to make the most of the weekend. Are you ready?"

"Yes."

"Then let's go."

The McKinney household, it had always seemed to Lori, pulsated with energy, but since Cynthia's arrival on the scene, a certain refinement had seeped into it. She had such flawless good taste and demanded the best of everything. But Cynthia was above all a smart woman who knew the kind of family she'd married into. For all the house's beauty, there was no touch-me-not elegance to it. It was a place meant to be lived in.

Cynthia was wearing a vivid green maternity outfit that went beautifully with her blond hair. She spent most of the evening seated in a chair near the fireplace, giving the impression she was holding court because she definitely was the center of attention. The family fawned over her solicitously, taking Lori's thoughts back to the arrival of the beautiful Bostonian at the Double C and the initial animosity J.T.'s family had shown her. What a difference a year—and the pending arrival of a new generation—could make.

Tonight almost everyone was present—Tyler and his wife Ruth, Cal and Serena, Lynn and Sam, Carolyn and Vernon. Only Beverly and Jeff Harris were missing. They had spent the day with friends at Lake Travis.

Lori was curious to see how Cody would interact with the McKinneys and how they would warm to him. He had told her he was acquainted with most of them, for they all did business with the bank, but he had never socialized with any of them. She watched in amusement as he "worked the room," making sure he spoke individually to everyone present. He was as casually self-confident with them as if he had known them his entire life. Of course he and Cynthia had plenty to talk about since both of them had spent their lives in banking circles. He even turned out to be knowledgeable about rodeo, so he and Cal had their heads together for a long time. He was really something to watch.

Lori made her way to the fireplace where Cynthia sat. "You look wonderful, Cynthia. How do you feel?"

"I feel fine, but my ankles swell if I stay on my feet very long. Thus, the chair. I'm really impressed with your date, Lori. I've met Cody several times, but this is the first chance I've had to really talk to him. What a charmer! How long have the two of you been seeing each other?''

''This is our fourth date.''

''Well, if I were you, I'd do whatever is necessary to keep him hanging around.''

''I intend to,'' Lori said.

After a delicious meal, the guests all filed into the living room where Virginia Parks was serving coffee. Most of the people present gathered near the hearth with its roaring fire, but Lori and Cody, finding no available seating, sat some distance away. They had no sooner been served their coffee than Hank put in an appearance, limping straight for Lori.

''Here comes Grandpa Hank,'' she told Cody in a lowered voice. ''He'll be a hundred on December twelfth. Expect anything.''

She jumped to her feet with a welcoming smile for the old man. Cody, too, stood and watched as the oldest person he had ever seen advanced on them, leaning heavily on a cane.

''Hank, it's wonderful to see you,'' Lori said brightly. ''Here, please take one of these chairs. I'll find another one.''

Hank sat down with some difficulty. He squinted up at Cody. ''Don't believe I know you, young feller.''

Cody grinned. It had been some time since anyone had referred to him as "young feller." "I'm Cody Hendricks, sir."

"Name's Hank Travis. Pardon my not gettin' up, but my hip gives me some trouble from time to time."

Lori, who had gone to find another chair, returned with one from the dining room. "Have the two of you met?" she asked.

"We just did," Cody said. He and Lori sat on either side of Hank, who was giving Cody a complete once-over.

"You're not from around here, are you?"

"No, sir. I'm from Houston."

"Houston, huh? What'd you do down there?"

"I was with the Oil and Gas Department of Southwest Bank."

A glimmer of interest lit up Hank's eyes. "Don't say. What'cha doin' here?"

"Cody's manager of the Crystal Creek branch now, Hank," Lori explained.

"Mmm." Hank hooked the cane over the arm of his chair, reached into his shirt pocket, withdrew some papers and a pouch of tobacco. He expertly rolled a cigarette and lit it. Exhaling smoke, he said, "I was in the oil bi'ness longer'n you been alive."

"Where did you work, sir?"

"All over the damned place. Oklahoma, East Texas, the Permian Basin. All over."

"Those must have been exciting days," Cody said.

"Yep. Man's work. Not like the prissy-pants operations they got goin' now. In those days, a man had to know what the hell he was doin'. Now all he's gotta know is how to push buttons. Nowadays drillers show up for work dressed like they's on their way to church." He leaned toward Cody conspiratorially. "Tell me somethin'—if I was to come to you wantin' to borrow some money to do a little prospectin', what would you say?"

Cody tried very hard to keep a straight face. He chanced a glance at Lori, who was fighting her own smile, then back at Hank.

"Well, sir, I…"

"Stop sir-in' me. My name's Hank."

"Well, Hank…first of all, I'd want to know where you intend drilling the well."

"On a couple'a acres an ol' drinkin' buddy of mine owned. Family's all gone now, and the land's just layin' there in Dimmit County."

"Dimmit? That's in the Austin Chalk."

"Damn right."

"So you're talking about a horizontal well."

Hank cackled. "Kills me, ever'body gettin' so damned excited about horizontal drillin', like it was just discovered last month. When I was in the oil patch it was called slant-holin' and was illegal as hell 'cause guys used it to suck up oil from other fellers' wells. Sure I'm talkin' about a horizontal well."

"All right," Cody said, being as businesslike as he could manage, "so assuming you could come up with a deed to the property, I'd want to see the geology of the area, the subsurface structure, Landsat imagery, that sort of thing. I'd want to know who was going to do the actual drilling and something about their track record in the business. I'd want to know how many investors you have and—"

Hank interrupted with an impatient snort. "You don't need any o' that BS. I've seen the oil."

Cody frowned. "Seen it? You mean, you've seen core samples or something like that?"

"No, I've *seen* the goddamn oil! Up here." He tapped his forehead.

Cody didn't know what to say. He looked at Lori and was astonished to see her nod her head in all seriousness, as though what the old man had said made perfect sense to her. Turning back to

Hank, he asked, "Do you have a survey of the property?"

"Yep, somewhere. Ol' Shorty gave it to me once for safekeepin'. He was awful bad about misplacin' stuff. Then he died...oh, 'bout twelve years ago. I tried to find some family, but I never could. Damned near forgot all 'bout the land until I had a dream."

"A dream?" Cody repeated.

"Yep. There's oil down there, all right. I've seen it. Oh, I know Beverly's young feller is drillin' on my land, but that's *his* deal. Our deal was that I would get lease payments and an override if they hit. I'm talkin' 'bout a last hurrah for *me*. Goddamn if it wouldn't be good to be around a bunch of oilers again! All ever'body around here wants to talk about is cows...and grapes." The last word was said with a sneer. It was common knowledge that Hank thought Tyler McKinney's venture into wine making was the silliest thing he had ever heard of, and he predicted dismal failure to anyone who would listen.

Now Hank, before Cody's dumbfounded eyes, pinched off the burning tip of his cigarette, put it in a nearby ashtray and pocketed the half-smoked stub.

"Yes, sirree," the old man said, more to himself than to Cody, "if I could just sit around some all-night café, drinkin' coffee, smokin' and listenin' to the chatter of half a dozen roughnecks…" A faraway look came to Hank's eyes. "If I could just do that for about a week, I could die a happy man."

At that moment there was some sort of commotion at the hearth. Lori looked over to see everyone on their feet, hovering over Cynthia.

"Why didn't you say something earlier, darling?" J.T. exclaimed. The color had drained from his face.

"Because it wasn't time to say anything, and I didn't want to spoil the party. The contractions have been coming all evening, but they've been widely spaced. Now they're coming more frequently, so I think it's about time—"

"Somebody call Dr. Purdy!" J.T. yelled, and Ruth ran out of the room.

"Is your bag packed?" Lynn asked anxiously.

"My bag has been packed for two weeks." Cynthia was the calmest person in the room.

Something had alerted Virginia, who bustled in. Taking stock of what was going on, she said, "I'll get the bag."

"Listen, everybody," Lynn said. "I think we ought to take as few cars as possible. You know what the parking situation at the hospital is. Tyler and Ruth can ride with Carolyn and Vern, and Cal and Serena can go with Sam and me, and…''

"Serena and I are going to have to take our car," Cal put in. "We're going back to Austin tonight."

"Wait a minute!" Tyler got everyone's attention. "I don't think we should create a mob scene at the hospital. I think Carolyn and Vern should go and Lynn go with them. The rest of us can wait here. We'll just be in the way."

Everyone seemed to agree with that. Amid much ado, J.T., Cynthia, Carolyn, Vernon and Lynn left. As Lynn passed her, Lori touched her arm. "Call me."

"Will do," Lynn promised.

At some point during all the confusion, Hank had dozed off. Lori signaled to Tyler, who crossed the room and touched the old man's shoulder. "Come on, Grandpa Hank. It's bedtime."

Hank roused and looked around. "Where'd ever'body go?"

"Daddy and Cynthia have gone to the hospital. The baby."

"Do tell." With some effort, he heaved himself out of his chair. Cody stood, too, and made a motion to help him, but it was brushed aside. "Be talkin' to you, young feller. You think about what I said.''

"I'll do that, Hank. Good night.''

A lull fell over the room. Virginia hurried in, collecting coffee cups. Ruth went to help her. "Anybody want a drink?" Cal asked. He and Sam made for the bar at the far end of the room.

Lori looked at Cody. "I think we should go.''

"I think so, too. This is a very private time.''

No one protested their leaving too much, knowing the vigil might be a long one and best done in the bosom of family. Outside, as Cody held the car door open for Lori, he said, "It's awfully early. Is there someplace you'd like to go?''

"Not that I can think of. Why don't we go to my house? There might be something on TV...or you might not have seen some of my videos. And I have a bottle of wine in the fridge that the man at the liquor store said is just dying to be noticed.'' She smiled. "Maybe we should go notice it.''

Cody grinned. "Sounds good to me." He shifted into gear and drove off. "Tell me something, Lori...do you think Hank really did see oil on that property?''

"Absolutely.''

"I thought so. I could tell by the look on your

face that you weren't having a bit of trouble with it. You know, it could have just been a dream, the kind ordinary people have all the time. That doesn't mean the oil's actually there.''

''Yes, it does,'' she said with a smile, ''because Hank doesn't have ordinary dreams. Oh, I know it's hard to believe, and there are plenty of people who think he's just a little tetched. But the McKinneys, Caro and I, Beverly—those of us who know him well—have just seen him proved right too many times to be skeptical.''

Cody gave that some thought. ''If anyone else told me that, I'd have my doubts, but you're perfectly sensible and rational, so I can't dismiss it as nonsense.''

''I could tell you plenty of stories,'' Lori said seriously. ''For instance, the morning Caro and I were in the bank and discovered money missing from her account…''

Cody tensed. ''Yes?''

''Only the night before, Hank had a dream that someone had stolen something from her.''

''That's…amazing.''

''Another instance. Last spring we had a real bad storm here in the Hill Country, the worst one in years. Hank had predicted it for weeks.''

''Oh, come on, Lori. The woods are full of old-timers who are forever correctly predicting the weather. They've been around so long they can pretty well tell when it's time for a big rain or whatever.''

''No, no, it wasn't his predicting the storm that was so incredible. It was something else. There's a woman who works the horses at the Circle T. Her name is Rosa Martinez, and she has a little girl, Teresa. Teresa had become attached to a dog named Bluebonnet, a dog Carolyn had taken in and nursed back to health after it was abandoned by the side of the road and struck by a car. Somehow Teresa got the mistaken notion that Carolyn was going to have Manny Hernandez put Bluebonnet to sleep, so she ran away with him. Then the storm hit, and the river flooded, and the little girl and the dog got caught out in it. Half of Claro County was out looking for them, but they'd about given up hope when Hank had one of his visions or dreams. He sent rescuers straight to them.''

Cody sat back and rubbed his chin thoughtfully. ''That's pretty incredible.''

''It was the most incredible thing I've ever personally seen.''

''Tell me something else, Lori…these visions of Hank's. Do they just come to him out of the blue, or are they prompted by things he's been thinking about for a while?''

She frowned in thought. ''I don't know. Maybe both. Why?''

''Oh…no reason. ESP, clairvoyance, things like that fascinate me.''

Lori chuckled. ''Cody, real bankers, *good* bankers aren't supposed to believe such things even exist.''

''I know.'' A bemused expression crossed Cody's face as he thought of his father and the bad time he gave him over Mary's ostrich farm. *Wonder what he'd have to say if I okayed a drilling loan because a hundred-year-old man ''saw'' oil on the property.*

He became aware that Lori was studying him. ''You don't remind me of a banker in any way,'' she said.

Smiling, he shot her a sideways glance. ''How many bankers have you known?''

''Just one.''

He smiled. ''Well, you don't remind me of an accountant, either, and I've known a bunch of those.''

The Circle T looked deserted and probably was. One lone light shone from a window in the main house, and there were none coming from the bunkhouse. Lori wondered if she and Cody were the only souls stirring on the place.

Inside Lori's house, Cody shrugged out of his jacket, tossed it on the back of an armchair and sat down on the sofa. Lori opened the folding doors that hid the kitchenette from view and withdrew a bottle of wine from the fridge. While she uncorked it and poured it into glasses, she said, "The TV listings are on top of the set."

"I'm not much for TV…unless there's a big game of some sort on."

"My videos are in that cabinet over there."

"Why don't we just talk? We have a long way to go toward getting really well acquainted."

"Suits me." She carried the glasses across the room, handed him one and sat down beside him. "I hope this lives up to its reputation. Are you a wine fancier?"

"Good Lord, no. I'm not even very particular about the brand of beer I drink."

Lori clinked her glass against his and took a sip. "Pretty good" was her verdict. "I'm not an expert, either. The man told me it had a full, fruity finish." She shrugged. "I'll take his word for it."

Cody lifted his glass to his lips and studied her over its rim. Lowering the glass, he said, "You're a very beautiful woman, Lori. Has anyone ever told you what incredible eyes you have?''

The statement took Lori's breath away. ''Well…I don't know. Seems like I would remember if anyone had.'' Cocking her head, she gave him an amused look. ''If that's not a line, it's just about the nicest thing I've ever heard.''

''I don't use lines. I wouldn't know how.''

''Then you don't deserve your reputation.''

Cody looked at her, puzzled. ''My reputation?''

''That you're a ladies' man.''

''You're kidding!''

''Not a bit.''

He gave that some thought. He was single and had been for some years, so he dated. He was positive deep in his heart that he had never done anything to make a woman think there was more to their relationship than actually existed. The term ''ladies' man'' bothered him enormously. It smacked of a man who used women for pleasure and little else. He hated it that Lori had heard something like that. ''I like the company of women,'' he said simply. ''I always have. I like the female viewpoint on life. It gives me a new perspective. Women tend to ponder and dissect things, seeing them from all angles. I hate to generalize, but *most* men see things in black and white, usually in connection with themselves. Do you know what men talk about when no women are present?''

"Women?''

"Ah, I figured that's what women think, but I'm going to destroy a myth right here and now. The conversation between a bunch of guys is pure vapid drivel—earned run averages, new car models, what a jackass an office superior is, the condition of the twelfth green. It's women who like to discuss interpersonal relationships. Men lean heavily toward Rambo-type conversations.''

"I'd never thought about it," Lori mused. "Of course, I haven't known all that many men really well. Family members, especially the DeMarcos. Now there's a macho bunch. I'll bet no man in that family has ever so much as rinsed out a cup, let alone conducted a 'meaningful' conversation with…well, with anybody. But other than my dad's family, there were a few boyfriends, then Michael.''

"Was he your first love?''

"Yes.''

There was a bite to Lori's voice that wasn't typical of her. "For some reason, I have the impression that the breakup wasn't amicable.''

"Hardly.''

"How long were you together?"

"Ten years."

"That's a long time," Cody remarked.

"Yes, but actually we were only married four years before disaster struck."

"Disaster?"

"Yes. She was blond."

"Yet you stayed with him six more years."

"It takes me a long time to own up to failure, I guess. I was married ten years, and Michael was married four. The blonde was just the first of several women."

Cody wondered whether being involved with a philanderer had colored her perception of men in general. "What about the coach?"

"Lou?" She was startled that Cody knew anything about Lou.

"Yes. You were dating him when I first arrived in Crystal Creek, as I recall."

He'd noticed? "Lou and I were little more than friends. I don't think either of us ever thought the relationship would be permanent. I know I didn't."

"Isn't it odd that we both have reached, roughly, midlife having had only one serious relationship? There aren't many like us around."

"By today's standards, I'm practically a virgin.'' Lori twisted toward him and propped an elbow on the back of the sofa. ''You've been alone a long time.''

''Yes, I have. You know…you remind me of Joanne in a lot of ways.''

''Your wife?''

''Yes.''

Good Lord, she thought. *Is that why he asks me out? How discouraging!*

''She was dark-haired, very sweet and pretty,'' Cody added.

Well, that helps some. ''You'll be happy to know you don't remind me of Michael at all.''

''How come?''

''For one thing, you seem to be a man of ambition. Michael wasn't, not even a little bit. He was a salesman for an electronics firm, and he had the gift of gab to make a good one. But he was more interested in making sure he could play golf every weekend. I sat by and watched other men in the company get ahead while he stagnated. If I had been in his shoes, that would have bothered me tremendously, but I don't think he cared in the least, just as long as he didn't miss any vacation time.''

''And for another?''

She studied him seriously. ''I realize we don't

know each other well, Cody, but instinct tells me you'd never allow your wife to be humiliated and made to feel undesirable.''

A smile touched the corners of his lips. ''Thanks for the vote of confidence. And I can't imagine what kind of creep would let you think for a minute you're undesirable. You well may be the most desirable woman I've ever met.''

Lori felt her insides melt. It had been so long since she'd heard talk like that she'd forgotten how a woman was supposed to respond to it. Not, she was sure, with the wide-eyed, gaping, school-girl expression she felt on her face at that moment. ''I...ah, that's a nice thing to say.''

''Only the truth.''

The arm resting on the sofa dropped as she saw him inch closer to her. He gave her a torturously slow, methodical kiss that sent waves of heat coursing through her. He kissed her mouth, her eyes, the tip of her nose, then her mouth again. ''Lori,'' he murmured huskily. ''You have the strangest effect on me. It's the damnedest thing I've ever felt.''

Lori noticed the amber liquid in her glass undulating slightly. She placed the glass on the coffee table and clasped her hands together. ''In... what way?''

"Well, it's not easy to explain. It—"

There was a knock at the door. Lori frowned, mumbled "Who on earth?" and got to her feet to answer it. To her surprise, Beverly and Jeff Harris stood on the stoop. "What are you doing here? We thought you were with your friends at the lake. Come in."

Beverly preceded Jeff into the room and did a little double take when she saw Cody, who was getting to his feet. "Hi, Cody."

"Hello, Beverly."

"Have you met Jeff Harris?"

"I believe we did meet once last summer." Cody stepped forward and offered his hand. "Nice to see you again."

Jeff looked a trifle uncertain about their having met before, but he shook Cody's hand, smiled and said, "Nice to see you, too."

Beverly turned to Lori. "Where are Mama and Vern? We drove by the Double C, but their car isn't there. Neither is J.T.'s Cadillac. And just as we passed the place, we saw Cal and Serena driving off. Did the party break up early?"

"Yes, because the hostess went into labor. Caro, Vern and Lynn are at the hospital."

Beverly clapped her hands together. "How exciting! A new cousin. Come on, Jeff, let's go to the hospital.''

"Why?" he asked. "So we can sit around waiting for a baby to be born?"

"Tyler suggested we not create a mob scene at the hospital," Lori said.

"Then what are we going to do?" Beverly asked Jeff.

"Do we have to do something?"

Lori was surprised by that remark. Surely by now Jeff knew that, yes, Beverly had to "do" something every waking minute. Resigned to company whether she wanted it or not, she shot Cody a vaguely apologetic look and said the last thing she wanted to say. "Cody and I were having a glass of wine. Would you like to join us?"

"Do you have beer instead?" Jeff asked.

"Yes."

"I'd rather have that."

"You, Bev?"

"Beer for me, too, thanks."

Lori was getting the beer out of the fridge when her astonished ears picked up the sound of another knock on the door. *What is this?* she wondered. She stayed out here night after night for months and no one came by. Why tonight? "Get that, will you, Bev?"

"Sure."

The new visitors were Brock and Amanda. Beverly asked them inside. "Where are your mom and Vern?" Amanda asked. "We were on our way back from town and thought we'd stop for a minute."

"Cynthia's having her baby. They're at the hospital," Beverly explained. "Come on in. We're all just waiting for some news."

Amanda and Brock stepped into the room. "Hello, Cody," Brock said in greeting. "How're things going?"

"Pretty good, thanks."

"Do you know Amanda Walker?"

"I don't believe I do. Hello, Amanda."

Greetings were exchanged all the way around, and drinks were passed. Normally Lori would have considered the impromptu get-together a pleasant diversion, but tonight she would have given anything simply to be alone with Cody. They exchanged glances from time to time, the message in his eyes clearly telling her that was what he wanted, too, but apparently it wasn't to be...not for some time at least.

But everyone was feeling talkative, and the conversation flowed amicably. Lori, Cody and Amanda polished off the bottle of wine, and more beer came out of the fridge for the others. Some time later, when the phone in Lori's bedroom rang, all eyes flew toward the sound. Lori jumped to her feet and ran to answer it, but when she returned, she shook her head. "That was Mary Gibson. A friend who works at the hospital called to tell her Cynthia had been admitted to Maternity. She just wanted to know if we'd heard anything."

Finally, it was Brock who made the first move to break up the gathering. Looking at his watch, he stood and held out his hand to Amanda. "I'm enjoying the heck out of this, but Amanda and I rise with the roosters these days. Guess we'll say good-night."

The group dispersed quickly. After saying good-night, Lori closed the door and turned to find Cody slipping on his jacket. "Must you go?"

"I think so. I have a feeling that's not the last time that phone's going to ring tonight." Smiling, he walked to her and rested his hands lightly on either side of her waist. "What will you do tomorrow?"

"Saturday's just another working day for me. But if the baby comes tonight, I'll probably go into town to pay a call on the new mother."

"Nothing but the drive-in windows are open

tomorrow, but I usually work in my office until two or so. If you do come into town, why don't you stop by the bank when you're finished with your business? We'll see what kind of trouble we can get into.''

Lori knew with certainty she was going to go into town tomorrow under some pretext or another. ''Fine. How will I get in?''

''There's an entrance in the rear with a bell. Just push the button and I'll be down.''

''Okay. I'm not sure what time it will be.''

''It doesn't matter.''

One of his hands moved to the side of her neck, and he looked at her with a kind of quiet intensity that took Lori's breath away. The searching silence seemed to go on forever. Then he bent his head; his mouth found hers and moved against her lips in a hot kiss. Everything inside Lori softened; her bones seemed to have melted. She leaned into the kiss, encouraging him to deepen it. She loved the way his mouth felt, the texture of his skin against her cheek, the brush of his hair at her temples.

At last he broke the kiss. She opened her eyes, and her breath escaped in a sound that was less than a moan, more than a sigh.

"Tomorrow," he said huskily. "Don't make any plans. We'll play it by ear."

"Y-yes."

The phone in her bedroom rang. Lori was hardly aware of it. She was still staring transfixed at his handsome face. Cody glanced pointedly toward the sound. "Maybe that's the news you've been waiting for. I'll let myself out. Good night, Lori."

"Good night." She stumbled into the bedroom and grabbed for the phone. "Yes?" she said, sounding as though she had been running.

"Lori, Lynn. I didn't wake you, did I?"

"Oh…no, Lynn. No."

"You don't sound like yourself. Cynthia just had a little girl, seven pounds, two ounces. Jennifer Travis. Little J.T. Is that cute or what?"

Lori was beginning to bring herself under control. "Oh, Lynn, how wonderful! Mother and baby are fine, I trust."

"Perfect. And Daddy's cooking on all four burners."

"Give them my love, and tell Cynthia I'll be in to see her tomorrow."

"Will do. Well, I have to go. I have about two dozen phone calls to make. Good night."

"Good night, Lynn. Thanks for calling."

Lori hung up, went to the bed and sank to its edge. She laughed a little shakily and placed her hand over her heart, as though that would calm its erratic beating. She didn't think the pulsating excitement inside her had a thing to do with Jennifer Travis McKinney's debut into the world. Lori was forty years old, and she felt exactly the way she had in high school the night Ted Moseley kissed her after the Halloween dance—as though she had just discovered something rare and wonderful that the rest of the world knew nothing about.

If she wasn't careful, she would fall in love. And she still knew almost nothing about Cody.

CHAPTER EIGHT

THE FOLLOWING MORNING, Lori was in the bathroom, sipping coffee and getting ready for the day, when her phone rang. Crossing her bedroom, she answered it. "Lori Porter."

"Lori?"

"Grandma?"

"Listen to me, darling. I've been thinking about that man you said you've been seeing. The banker."

Lori smiled. "I'll just bet you have."

"My instincts tell me you've finally found the right one."

Lori's smile broadened. "Oh, Grandma, you know nothing about him. Your instincts tell you I've found a banker."

"You said you like him."

"Yes, he's very nice. You'd like him too."

Anna uttered a gasp. "Will you bring him to meet me?"

"Well...maybe one of these days. We'll just have to see how things go between us."

"You're seeing him again soon, I hope."

"Yes, as a matter of fact, I'm meeting him this afternoon."

"What are the two of you going to do?"

"I'm not sure. He asked me to meet him this afternoon and we'd decide what we wanted to do."

"Oh, that's wonderful! You know, darling...I've been thinking that I really should have my mink coat altered to fit you. I mean, you're going out with a banker now, so you should dress the part."

Oh, Lord! Anna had been dangling that coat in front of the females in the family for years, and it had never gotten through to her that no one wanted the thing. But since the mink was one of Anna's proudest possessions, a great deal of tact had to be employed when refusing it. "A mink coat would be totally inappropriate in Crystal Creek, Grandma. It's just not a mink coat type of place. Besides, what if Cody turned out to be an animal rights activist or something?"

"Mmm, I hadn't thought of that. Well, I'll let you get ready for your date with your young man.

And listen to me, Lori—don't do anything to discourage him.''

"I won't. Promise."

"Goodbye, darling."

Chuckling, Lori returned to the bathroom to finish dressing.

CRYSTAL CREEK CAME ALIVE on Saturdays. It was the day all the area's ranchers and farmers came to town to do their shopping. Today not even overcast skies and threatening weather kept the people away. Street crews were out putting the traditional Christmas decorations on the streetlights, as well as stringing lights on the big tree in the courthouse square. Since this was the first weekend after Thanksgiving, most of the downtown shops were crowded. Berne's Drugstore and Gift Shop was one such place. After visiting Cynthia at the hospital, Lori stopped at the drugstore to pick up some items for Carolyn and Beverly. She was moving up and down the aisles, consulting her list, when she spotted a familiar blond head.

"Hello, Mary Alice."

Mary Alice turned. "Hi, Lori. Oh, am I glad I ran into you today." She closed the space between them and lowered her voice. "I'd like you to do a favor for me."

"A favor? All right."

"You know all that stuff I told you about Luke and me, about getting married and all?"

"Yes."

"I'd really like it if you didn't mention it to anyone. Luke doesn't want it to get around yet."

Of course he doesn't, Lori thought sourly, *because chances are good it isn't going to happen.* "All right, Mary Alice, I won't say a word." It was rather like locking the barn door after the horse had been stolen, she realized, because she'd already told Cody. But there was no harm there. Cody couldn't possibly be one iota interested in Mary Alice's love life.

"Thanks a bunch. I really appreciate it. Well, I guess I'd better get moving. Luke's waiting for me. See you."

"Goodbye, Mary Alice." Lori watched the young woman walk away and shook her head sadly. If only there were some way of warning her. Shaking off the thought, she finished her shopping and carried her selections to the cash register, where Janet Wall, the pharmacist's daughter, greeted her.

"Hello, Lori. Looks like we're in for some rain."

"Something we don't need, not after last month."

Janet began ringing up Lori's purchases. "You know, my cousin Betty works at the country club, and she said you went to the Thanksgiving dance with Cody Hendricks."

"Yes, I did."

"Lord, he's a good-looking one."

Lori merely smiled.

"Poor Emma Clark had such a case on him last summer. He dated her a few times, then nothing. I thought she was going to pine away."

"Janet, I really don't want to hear—"

"I don't know anyone he's dated more than a couple of times. Must be the love-'em-and-leave-'em type. That's twenty-two ninety-five."

Lori paid for her purchases, scooped up the sack and left the store, Janet's voice ringing in her ears. As she headed for her car, she noticed Luke sitting in a battered pickup parked a couple of spaces away from her. The man almost made her ill. But as sorry as she felt for Mary Alice, Lori wondered if perhaps she shouldn't start being more concerned about something closer to home.

INSIDE THE STORE, Mary Alice moved quickly up and down the aisles, selecting her purchases and putting them in a shopping basket. She paid for the things Luke had told her he needed—razor blades, after-shave, shaving cream, deodorant—then hurried to the truck parked in front of the store. She placed the sack on the seat between them. "I think I remembered everything," she said. "I hope the brands are okay."

Luke straightened in the seat. "Thanks, sugar. Sorry I got caught without any money. Is the receipt in the sack? I'll pay you back as soon as I cash a check." He switched on the engine and shifted into reverse.

"Don't be silly, Luke. You don't have to pay me back. It's all going to be coming out of the same pot pretty soon anyway. It isn't really my money. It's our money."

They slowly drove through the crowded streets. As they passed Southwest Bank, Mary Alice noticed Mr. Hendricks's car in the executives' parking lot at the rear of the building. In fact, there were a lot of cars in the parking lot. The employees were decorating the bank for Christmas that afternoon. Mary Alice felt guilty about not being there, but she wouldn't let anything interfere with even one minute she could spend with Luke.

Driving past the bank reminded her of something. "Are you sure we can get along fine without my paycheck, Luke? I've been with the bank a long time. I wouldn't have any trouble getting a bank job in Fort Worth."

"We'll get along just dandy," Luke said without much feeling.

Mary Alice wished she could be so sure. But he'd once told her she was going to be helping him out on the ranch and wouldn't have time to have another job. Still, the thought of no paycheck bothered her from time to time.

When it did, however, she would remind herself that her life was going to change drastically. It would be very different from her mother's. Mary Alice had seen firsthand how difficult and lonely life was when a woman didn't have a man to help her out. To have to go through life alone was just about the worst thing she could imagine. Every day she blessed whatever fate had sent Luke her way.

Yet, she was greatly troubled by something else. "I sure hate to quit without giving the bank notice. It just doesn't seem right somehow. I ought to be there to train a new teller."

"Naw, don't say anything about quitting, not yet. Something might happen to delay our plans."

"Like what?" A tingle of fear rose inside Mary Alice. She couldn't bear to think of a delay.

Luke only shrugged. "Junk happens. It's best to cover your bases. Besides, you don't owe that ol' bank anything. You've worked for years for peon's wages as it is. If they don't like you quitting on the spur of the moment, tell 'em to shove it."

Mary Alice shifted in her seat, looking at him with a smile. She knew there were those who thought him cocky and arrogant, but she didn't see him that way at all. To her, Luke epitomized self-confidence, something she sadly lacked. She was always worried about offending people, doing or saying something that would hurt feelings or step on toes. Luke didn't care what people thought. It seemed to her it would be wonderful to go through life that way.

Settling against the back of the seat, she crossed her arms under her breasts. The thought of getting married was so exciting, but she wished it didn't have to be hush-hush, then done in a hurry. Although she was thrilled about the turn her life had taken, thanks to Luke, she still felt a little cheated.

All her life she had dreamed of a church wedding. She'd always known it couldn't be a fancy one, but how she would love to have everyone she knew come to see her actually become Mrs. Luke Harte. Not once in her life had she been the center of attention, as were all brides at traditional marriages, at least for an hour or so. And perhaps she wanted to enjoy the luxury of gloating a little. Not one of her high school friends had married a man as good-looking as Luke.

"Luke, are you sure we can't have a real wedding? I've saved five hundred dollars. I know that's not much, but it would be enough for Mama's friend Kate to make me a pretty dress. And enough for flowers, maybe cake and punch. Kate's husband is a pretty good photographer. He wouldn't charge us to take some pictures."

Luke looked horrified. "Five hundred dollars for something that's over in fifteen minutes? That's the stupidest waste of money I can think of. Naw, you hold on to that money. There'll be lots better places to put it, lots better."

"Well, for sure I think Mama should put the house on the market right away. She says anything she gets for it is going to us, as her way to thank us for letting her live with us. It'd be awful nice to have that money when we're starting out."

Luke knew it would be a major miracle if that house sold without a face-lift. The outside was a mess. He could do most of what needed doing, but he wasn't inclined to. And for sure he didn't intend spending any of his own money paying someone else to do it. "You worry about the damnedest things, Mary Alice. I told you, wait until we're sure when we're leaving. What if the house sold right away and we couldn't leave for Fort Worth for weeks? What would you and your mom do then? It's no big deal if we move away and the house is still on the market. Save your worrying for heavy stuff."

Mary Alice sighed. Maybe he was right. He sure seemed to think he was. Getting married and moving away was such a big event in her life, but Luke was taking it all very casually. He hadn't even bought her wedding ring yet, saying there was plenty of time for that. She guessed men just looked at things like marriage and weddings differently. For sure Luke was sometimes a real mystery to her. She sighed again and looked out the window.

Luke drove into the Priests' driveway, then glanced at Mary Alice out of the corner of his eye. He hated it when she got all glum and serious. He especially hated it when she started all that wedding talk. Women were funny creatures. He wasn't sure men were even supposed to understand them.

Reaching out, he cupped her chin, forcing her to look at him. "Tell you what. Why don't you put on your honky-tonk duds and let me take you to Zack's tonight?"

"I thought we couldn't afford to do stuff like that."

"Sure we can...at least once in a while."

"Sounds like fun."

Luke gave her a playful nudge and a warm smile. Mary Alice blushed and smiled shyly. Did it really matter what kind of wedding they had?

LORI PUSHED the doorbell button at the bank's back entrance. In a few seconds the door opened, and Cody stood grinning at her. "Hello," he said.

"Hello," she replied, grinning as broadly as he was and conveniently forgetting what Janet had said.

"Did Cynthia have her baby?"

"Oh, yes. It was Lynn who was calling when you left last night. A little girl. Jennifer Travis."

"Mother and baby are fine, I hope." He took her arm and ushered her inside.

"Splendid. They're going home Monday morning. Cynthia doesn't look as though she's done anything more strenuous than thumb through magazines."

They stepped into the waiting elevator, and Cody pushed a button. A soft whirring sound accompanied their ascent. Lori had expected the bank to be quiet as a tomb on Saturday afternoon, but it was buzzing with activity. An enormous evergreen had been placed in the center of the lobby, and half a dozen people stood on ladders decorating it. Others were stringing garlands and ribbons along the railings and the tellers' cages.

"Personally," Cody said, "I think putting up Christmas decorations the weekend after Thanksgiving is rushing the season a bit, but I'm told that's when the bank always does it."

"And it always looks so beautiful when it's done. Very elegant for Crystal Creek."

He eyed the stadium jacket she wore over her sweater and slacks. "Has it gotten colder?"

"A lot. The cold front must have come through. And it's beginning to mist."

"Come on into the office. I'm just finishing up some work."

It seemed strange to see him in these surroundings dressed in jeans and a plaid shirt. No matter what he wore, he exuded an air of virility.

A stack of folders stood in the center of his desk. Cody quickly stashed all but one in a drawer. "I'm going in there to wash up," he said, nodding in the direction of his private lavatory, "and then we'll leave."

While she waited, Lori idly roamed the office, then stopped to peer out the window behind his desk. It was a miserably gray day, and it had begun to rain. When she turned, the folder on his desk caught her eye. Personnel File was printed in black on the front, and the name written on its tab caught her eye. Mary Alice Priest. And on the front of the folder there was a stick-on note. *Ralph,* the note read, *new info. Check it out. This might be something.*

Lori frowned, but at that moment the lavatory door opened, and Cody stepped out, smiling. "Ready?"

"Yes. Where are we going?"

"Have you had lunch?" he asked, reaching for a pile-lined denim jacket.

"No."

"Then how about a bite at the Longhorn Coffee Shop?"

"Sounds great."

Cody picked up the folder on the desk, tucked it under his arm, and they left the office. Outside in the corridor, he stopped and peered over the railing. "Ralph," he called.

A man on one of the ladders turned around. "Yes, Cody?"

"I have something I want you to look at before you leave." He held up the folder. "I'll put it on your desk."

"Fine."

To Lori Cody said, "Give me a second." She watched him enter an office similar to his own, only much smaller. He put the folder on the desk, then rejoined Lori in the corridor. "All set."

They walked to the elevator. Lori vaguely wondered why Mary Alice was being singled out. Maybe, she thought hopefully, her friend was being considered for a promotion. That would be wonderful. A promotion and raise would do wonders for her self-esteem. But more important than that, they just might lessen Luke's importance in Mary Alice's life.

BY THE TIME Lori and Cody finished lunch, the rain was coming down in silvery sheets. "Cold and wet," she muttered. "My least favorite kind of weather."

"I know," he agreed. "What can you do on a day like this?" Naturally Cody could think of a perfect way to spend a rainy day, but he wisely decided it was neither the time nor the place to mention it. He briefly considered asking her to come to his place, but remembered it was was pretty messy. His cleaning woman came on Tuesdays, and he could do a lot of damage by the weekend.

Lori dreamily recalled the early days of her marriage when cuddling up in front of a fire on a day like this was her idea of cozy heaven. She had been very much in love, but that was long ago—a lifetime, it seemed. Now she had found a man who could make her senses sing again. "We could go to my house," she said, trying to keep her voice light. "I've got a wood-burning stove, so we can have a fire. I can make hot chocolate, we can maybe watch a movie, and I have plenty of groceries for dinner."

Cody looked slightly dazzled. "Talked me into it. Sounds perfect. I'll take you to your car, then follow you."

They both got slightly damp during the dash to Cody's car, Lori damper still when they returned to the bank and she sprinted for hers. And by the time they got through her front door, both their jackets were sopping wet.

"Give yours to me," Lori said as she shrugged out of hers. "I'll hang them on the shower rod to dry. Would you build a fire? I think the stove has wood in it.''

It turned out to be a perfect afternoon. Lori made hot chocolate, and they drank from steaming mugs while seated on the floor in front of the now blazing fire. They talked about everything, and they talked about nothing in particular. Lori gently questioned Cody about his family but got only monosyllables for answers. She wondered if he didn't get along with them particularly well. He avoided her questions so skillfully that she soon found herself talking about her family, her childhood. Finally, the talk got around to Lori's grandmother.

''She was so-o-o strict. Both of my parents worked, so I spent a lot of time with Grandma. She'd never had a daughter, and there I was— fresh clay to be molded and shaped into her idea of perfection. My education was entrusted to the sisters at Sacred Heart. I was in church every single Sunday. She constantly reminded me that once they were past fifteen, men were interested in 'only one thing.''' Lori rolled her eyes. ''I used to feel sorry for the young fellows who came to our house. I mean, a poor guy might be there wanting me to help with his algebra, but he got such a grilling. It's funny. The only time Grandma didn't worry about me was during the ten years I was married to Michael, and that's when she should have worried the most.''

''I suppose she wanted you to 'marry well.' ''

''Lord, yes. If I could just find myself a millionaire, Grandma could die happy. I finally had to tell her she was wasting her wishing. I'm a middle-class girl with middle-class values. I wouldn't have the first idea how to act around a millionaire.''

''Well, Lori, I...I would think you could just be yourself.''

''I doubt that. I used to work for a big accounting firm in San Antonio, and it had a lot of wealthy clients. They were just...different. I told my superior that once, and she said the rich *are* different and that's why they keep to their own kind.''

She was staring at the fire and so did not see the troubled look that came over Cody's face.

''LORI, THAT WAS without question the best lasagna I've ever eaten,'' Cody said, scooping up the last bite. Not only had they each consumed big helpings of the dish, they had made a considerable dent in a loaf of French bread and a bottle of Beaujolais.

"Glad you liked it."

"Now," Cody said with satisfaction, looking at her over the rim of his glass, "we have a long, lazy night ahead of us."

He might have meant a lot by that, or nothing at all. Lori didn't even know what time it was, and she felt no particular urge to search out a clock. The rain was still a torrent, but inside the little house, all was warm and cozy. And she was awash in contentment.

Picking up their plates and silverware, she carried them to the sink, quickly rinsed them and left them for washing later. She refilled their glasses and carried them to the coffee table. Cody was in front of the stove, studying the fire. He threw in another log; a shower of sparks sputtered behind the glass.

Lori sat on the sofa and within seconds he had joined her, sliding one arm along her shoulders. She turned in his arms, and their eyes met. The combination of his lazy smile and those eyes did crazy things to her senses. She knew exactly what she wanted to happen between them, but she wasn't sure when it should happen. However, if he kept looking at her like that, the decision probably wouldn't be made with her head but her heart.

"This is nice," she murmured.

"Yes, it is. That was a wonderful meal."

"Thanks. It's been a wonderful afternoon, actually."

"Isn't it funny that sometimes just doing nothing is most fun of all? By the way, I couldn't sleep when I got home last night, so I finally got around to reading that book."

"Which one?"

"The aliens with the black tails."

"Oh, *The Sulange Warriors.*"

Cody inched closer to her, and the hand resting lightly on her shoulders dropped. "By the way, it was the hero's thigh, not his waist, that the heroine wrapped her tail around...and squeezed hard."

Lori smiled, feeling her face warm. "Well, it's been some time since I read it."

"Personally, my favorite part was when they disappeared into the mating tent to live on nothing but water and body fat. And emerged sixteen days later with the emaciated look of lovers who had mated properly."

The hand on her shoulders drew her to him and ran down her arm, coming to rest at her waist. "I don't think you'd last sixteen days, Lori. Not enough body fat."

Laying her head on his shoulder, she laughed lightly. "But remember, they feasted for sixteen days before going into the tent."

"Sounds rather rigorous to me."

"The feasting or the tent?"

"Both." Gently Cody slid his free arm around her waist, enveloping her in an embrace. He then kissed her deeply until she was breathless. When he lifted his head, hers went back, she closed her eyes, and let out a sigh.

"You make me want to say the damnedest things," he confessed in a husky voice.

"Like what?"

"Oh…nonsense about raining rose petals and lilacs at your feet."

"Good grief!" Lori exclaimed, truly amazed that there was a living, breathing man left in the universe who would say something like that.

"Blather about wanting to make you happier than you've ever been in your life."

"Oh, my God!" Impulsively, she placed both her hands on his thigh and squeezed as hard as she could. "In the absence of a long, black, whip-like tail, will this do?"

"Oh, Lori."

They sat, embracing tightly for a minute. Then Cody pulled away slightly. "You are very, very special to me. It's important to me that you believe that.''

Lori had never wanted to believe anything more. "I'm here, aren't I?''

"So you are.''

"It's been such a long time for me.''

"Believe it or not, it's been quite a while for me, too.''

From that moment on, his lips and hands were never still. Lori realized she had forgotten what this was like, the pure pleasure of it. It was like nothing else on earth—the intensity of emotion, the rush of hot blood through the veins, the desire to fuse, meld, mesh with another human being. While Cody's lips and hands worked their magic, she felt herself transported to a wonderland of enchantment where she was beautiful, desirable, loved. She felt like a *woman* again, and it was a feeling to be savored above all others.

Cody lifted his head. His eyes, usually so open and warm, were dark, stormy, emotion-filled. Struggling to his feet, he pulled her up with him. He glanced pointedly toward the door to her bedroom. "Come with me. I know a much better place for this sort of thing.''

If Lori experienced even one hesitant thought about the direction this was going, she couldn't remember it later. She merely followed him, her heart pounding like a thousand drums. The minute they crossed the threshold, Lori was in his arms again. His fingers slithered through her hair, then dropped to her shoulders to caress her gently. His touch was courtly, worshipful, and a little shiver ran through her body. Seeing it, feeling it, Cody smiled, cupped her face in his hands and grazed her mouth with his, then her earlobe and the underside of her chin.

A sigh escaped Lori's lips. Overcome by a warm willingness, she melted against him until their bodies fit together like pieces of a puzzle.

Abruptly Cody turned toward the bed, and with one fluid motion he pulled down the spread. Straightening, he held out his arms, and she went into them. Raising a hand to unbutton her blouse, Lori felt his detain her.

"This we'll do together," he said huskily.

And so, rather clumsily and impatiently, they undressed each other; then Cody took her in his arms and they sank down onto the bed. She stroked his face, staring at him in wonder. Desire made him even more handsome, and she wouldn't have thought that possible. Not only that, he was as trim and firm as a much younger man. She reveled in the feel of his hands touching every part of her. There had been so many times in the past when she had feared that her sexuality was dead forever, but now she knew better. Every part of her body was alive and tingling with sensations. She matched Cody touch for touch, kiss for kiss, demand for demand. His whispered endearments were music to her ears. She was on fire, and she wanted to wallow in the pure physical pleasure of it. Now she remembered that a woman felt a certain sense of pride in knowing she could arouse a man. With his strong body covering hers and her legs binding him like loving ropes, she felt every inch of her femininity.

Yet even in the throes of the first passion she had experienced in years, she was sufficiently aware to realize he was an expert lover—practiced, perfect. He knew exactly what to say, where to touch. He had mastered the art of lovemaking.

Then he entered her, and they caught the rhythm, moving together with the ease of long-time lovers. Lori wanted it to go on forever, but inevitably, the golden fire began to spread from the core of her femininity. Her fingernails bit into his shoulder as she cried out his name. The minute her climax began, she felt Cody withdraw from her, and in a violent burst of passion, they both were completed.

For several minutes afterward, Cody's body remained on top of hers, pressing her into the mattress. She stroked his back and kissed his shoulder, smiling secretly to herself. Maybe in days to come she would have reason to regret tonight, but for now, everything seemed very right.

When he rolled off her, he pulled her to him, tucking her against his side. "Ah, Lori, you are fantastic!"

"You're pretty frisky. You make me feel eighteen again. Well...almost." Lori snuggled against him. "Oh, this feels so nice. Being in your arms is like being wrapped in a snug, warm, safe cocoon."

"I hope it always feels that way."

"And you know something? I choose not to become a butterfly. I'm going to remain a plain little caterpillar so I can stay here...and stay and stay."

CHAPTER NINE

THE RAIN WAS STILL coming down hard when Lori woke the next morning. She quietly slipped out of bed, not disturbing Cody, and put on her robe. After brushing her teeth and combing her hair, she went to the kitchen to make coffee. Last night's dishes were still in the sink, so while the coffee was brewing, she washed them and put them away, then opened the blinds in the living room and peered out.

The ground was a loblolly. Ever since the big flood in the spring, the water had been higher than usual in the Claro River. If it overflowed its banks, the ranch could be cut off from town. These Hill Country toad-stranglers were something to behold!

She went to the bedroom door and peeked in. Cody was still sleeping soundly. ''I'm wasted'' was the last thing he'd said before they both fell asleep for good, sometime after midnight. It had been such a glorious, love-filled night. At one point she had conveniently shaken off the reminder that she still had reservations about him. Being with him had just been too wonderful.

At that moment, Cody stirred. Rolling over, he stretched and yawned. Lori quickly went to the kitchen and poured a cup of coffee, then carried it to the bedside and wafted it back and forth under his nose. His eyes flew open.

"Is that a way to be wakened or what?" he exclaimed.

"Drink it while it's hot. I'm taking breakfast orders. I have orange juice, tomato juice, cinnamon rolls, bacon, eggs, biscuits...."

"What a treat." He took the cup from her hand and sipped.

"I apologize for the unadorned morning face," she said.

"That morning face looks damned good to me, Lori. I apologize for the stubble."

She studied his face a minute. "The stubble's kind of attractive. It makes you look masculine, rough and ready...used."

"Well, I certainly feel used this morning."

"Have you ever worn a beard?"

He pretended to be shocked. "Please, Lori, I'm a banker."

"Bankers don't wear beards?"

"None I've ever known."

"A mustache then?"

"Once."

"You didn't like it?"

He shook his head. "I hated it. Those things are a pain in the posterior." He curved his free hand behind her nape, pulled her head down and brushed his lips against her temple. "Fix whatever you want for breakfast. At home, if I eat at all, it's cereal."

She sat on the edge of the bed next to him. "Tell me about your house."

"It's just...a house. Three bedrooms, two baths...you know, standard stuff. If this blasted rain would stop, I'd take you to see it today."

"When you lived alone in Houston, did you have a bachelor pad?"

"Sort of." His bachelor pad had been a penthouse apartment big enough to go quail hunting in. He'd lived in maybe a third of it. It had been Park Avenue elegant and as warm and homey as a mausoleum. He could really live in the house he had now.

"Were you a swinging bachelor?" she teased.

"Never. Besides, I wasn't a bachelor. I was a widower."

If she wanted him to clam up, Lori noticed, all

she had to do was ask him about Houston. Pivoting, she said, "I'll have breakfast ready in no time. There are new toothbrushes in the top drawer left of the basin."

Cody gulped down his coffee and threw back the covers. He retrieved his jeans from the floor and stepped into them, not bothering with his shorts. He slipped on his shirt but left it unbuttoned. Going into the bathroom, he scowled at his image in the mirror, then found a toothbrush. Some sort of funny-looking comb with widely spaced teeth was lying next to the basin. He ran it through his hair, but it didn't do much good. Shaving could wait, too, he decided. Turning, he went to join Lori.

Two glasses of orange juice sat on the table. He gulped down one and picked up yesterday's Austin paper. "I always go into town for the Sunday paper," Lori told him, "but I'm afraid there'll be none of that today."

"That's fine. I haven't read yesterday's."

Within minutes she had placed a tempting plate of ham, scrambled eggs and biscuits in front of him.

They ate in silence for a minute while Cody scanned the paper. All of a sudden Lori looked around and began giggling. Cody glanced up. "What's so funny?"

"Look at this," she said. "Cozy breakfast, a newspaper. Me without makeup and you un-shaved. Cody...do you realize that last night was only the fifth evening we've spent together. *Fifth!*"

"Do you think I'm moving too slow?" he asked with a grin.

She shook her head in amazement. "It's so un-like me."

"Then why last night?"

"Because...I think I had to get it out of my system."

"And did you?"

"I...don't think so."

"Good." Cody reached across the table and took her hand in his. "I've waited a hell of a long time for you to show up. I was beginning to think you weren't ever going to make it."

Lori smiled, then sobered. "That sounds nice, but you can't really know that, Cody. Not yet. All you can possibly know is how good we are in bed."

"Common sense would tell me the same thing, but it seems to have left me. I know."

"Don't tell me we were meant for each other."

"Maybe we were."

"I don't know much about you, you know."

"You know everything that's important."

Lori wondered. She wished her intuition would leave her alone and let her just enjoy this. She certainly wouldn't go so far as to say he was mysterious, but there was something about himself he kept from the world. She just knew it.

After breakfast, Cody plopped down on the sofa, picked up a magazine and began leafing through it. Lori refilled their cups, emptying the coffeemaker, then crossed the room and sat beside him. "May I ask you a question that's probably none of my business?"

"Sure."

"Yesterday when I was in your office, I happened to see Mary Alice's personnel folder lying on your desk. Naturally I was curious. Is she being singled out for something?"

Cody hesitated. He put the magazine back on the coffee table and glanced over at Lori. "You could say that, I guess."

"A promotion?"

"Not...exactly."

Lori sat back, frowning. "What else could she be singled out for?"

"Lori, I periodically go over the employees' personnel files."

"One at a time? And there was a note on it, something about new information."

"It's just bank business...dry and uninteresting."

"I must say you're being very mysterious about this. I was just asking a question about a friend. You're not...considering letting her go, I hope."

"I hope not, too."

"Oh, Cody, surely... Mary Alice and her mother need that job. It would be disastrous for them if she lost it. She's very loyal to the bank, isn't she? She has a superlative work record, doesn't she? She probably would mop floors after hours if you asked her to. I don't know how you could even consider letting her go."

A pained expression crossed Cody's face. "Well, you see, Lori... You know that two thousand that was missing from Carolyn's account? We never have found it."

Lori's frown deepened. "You haven't? Then why did you tell me you had?"

"I don't believe I ever told you that."

"Yes, you did. Last weekend at the book fair...I asked you, and you..." She paused, trying to remember what he'd actually said.

"And I did this." He made a circle with his thumb and index finger.

"Well, that certainly *implied* you'd found the money."

"Maybe."

"Why?"

"So you and Carolyn would forget it. I didn't want any talk going on. So far only six people know the money's missing—well, you make seven. It's pretty delicate business, Lori. Ralph and I have almost scratched our heads raw over it. We've spent two weeks dissecting the lives of everyone at the bank who handles money."

"Looking for what?"

"Almost anything that smacks of money problems."

"I daresay the only money problem poor Mary Alice has is lack of it." Lori picked up her cup and sipped. "Have you checked the personnel records of every teller?"

"Of course."

"Why would you single her out for closer scrutiny, her of all people—shy, retiring Mary Alice?"

"Still waters...and all that."

Lori considered that and dismissed it. "Forgive

me, but…baloney. There's more to this than you're telling me. Why Mary Alice?''

Cody sighed. ''I'm afraid that Mary Alice has come under the microscope because…because of her involvement with Luke Harte.''

Lori's eyes widened. She stared at him a few seconds before saying, ''Cody! Are you telling me you took things I said about a friend of mine and…are using them to implicate her in a theft?''

Something in the tone of her voice alerted Cody. ''I've investigated everyone, Lori—their financial records, their private lives. The only thing I keep coming back to is Luke's history of gouging money out of women. You've told me yourself how gullible Mary Alice is, how eager she is to please.''

''I don't believe this! I feel…betrayed.''

''Oh, come on. None of those things you told me were said in confidence, were they? I certainly don't recall….''

Lori jumped to her feet and began pacing the floor. ''I know Mary Alice didn't take that money.''

''No, you don't.''

''There's got to be a better way of finding out who did, something other than snooping and prying.''

"There probably is. Ideally, I'd get a confession, but a confession requires an accusation, and I have to be careful there. Or, I could catch the thief with a hand in the till, but apparently the two thousand is going to be it. Less ideally, I could have everyone's handwriting analyzed."

Lori stopped pacing and looked at him. "Handwriting?"

"That withdrawal slip I showed you has a bogus signature on it." Succinctly he explained the bank's policy. "I've personally checked every deposit and withdrawal slip since the theft was discovered."

"Then you have a sample of Mary Alice's handwriting."

"Afraid not. She prints her initials on her transactions. Inconclusive."

"Well, then, why don't you get all the handwritings analyzed?"

"I may have to, but for now I'd rather not. News like that spreads like wildfire, and I could find myself in some hot water."

"Why?"

"Because I took Carolyn's word for it that she hadn't made that withdrawal, without doing even the most basic amount of checking. There are plenty of bankers who wouldn't have." His father, for one. Robert. The Board members.

"So why did you?"

"Because I know and trust Carolyn."

"But you don't trust Mary Alice?"

Cody slowly shook his head. "Not now that I know about Luke."

Lori ran her fingers through her hair. "I wish I hadn't said a word."

Cody stood and went to put his arms around her waist. "Do you think it's all right for Mary Alice to get away with it...if indeed she did take the money?"

Lori faltered momentarily, then lifted her eyes and looked at him defiantly. "She didn't do it. I'm very intuitive about people, and I know she didn't take that money."

"I have a hunch she did...and I have no more reason to believe in her guilt than you do her innocence. Intuition and hunches are worthless."

"Leave her alone, Cody. *Please* just leave her alone."

His mouth set stubbornly, giving him a look Lori hadn't seen before. "I'm only doing my job, Lori," he said. "Now, let's drop it. Your coffee's getting cold."

BUT SHE DIDN'T drop it. She talked about it incessantly, during the time it took them to get dressed, while he shaved, even through lunch. Too late Cody realized he never should have admitted Mary Alice's involvement with Luke was the chief reason she was under such a heavy cloud of suspicion. This was hardly the way he had envisioned spending the day. Time and again he tried to change the subject, only to have it brought up again.

"Remember Viktor in *Twilight of the Lost World?*" she suddenly asked.

"What in hell does that have to do with anything?"

"Remember his favorite expression? 'Distrust the obvious.'"

Cody groaned. "Lori, will you drop it? I'm tired of talking about it!"

"I think it's just easier for you to pick on poor Mary Alice than to dig deeper."

"I'm not picking on anyone. I'm simply trying to get to the bottom of this before it turns into a major stink."

"Why the tellers?" Lori persisted stubbornly. "Why not some higher-ups?"

"It's too penny-ante, for one thing. Higher-ups usually embezzle big bucks. Two thousand dollars. Not even enough to get the law interested. And that's what's going to save her skin if she's guilty. A confession and restitution, and she's home free.''

Lori eyed him suspiciously. ''And just who's going to get a confession out of her? You?''

Cody shook his head. ''No. I could find myself with a real bag of worms if I accused her on a hunch.''

Lori took a deep breath. ''Possibly…me?''

That thought hadn't crossed Cody's mind until that minute, but it was a good possibility. ''Who else would she talk to so freely…so woman-to-woman?''

Lori's jaw dropped, and she stared at him in disbelief. Then she turned on her heel and disappeared into her bedroom. Cody clasped his hands in front of him and heaved a sigh. Silence lay over the house like a shroud. The only sound was the lashing of the rain against the windows.

Suddenly Lori reappeared in the doorway. ''Is that what all this has been about?''

Cody glanced up, uncomprehending. ''I don't understand.''

''The rush. A week's worth of dates when you never noticed me before. I was feeding you valuable information that you couldn't possibly have gotten anywhere else.''

The look on Cody's face was indescribable. He stood, pulling himself up to his full height, and glared at her. ''I can't believe you think that's true. If you do, you're an idiot.''

''You know, I really believed all that stuff you told me about how special I was.''

''I never said one word to you that wasn't the truth.'' He all but spit out the words. Crossing into the bathroom, he returned carrying his jacket, and strode purposefully toward the door. ''I'm going home. I've had about enough of this. Thanks for lunch.'' The front door slammed solidly behind him.

For a long time after he'd left, Lori stood in the doorway and gazed unseeingly at the rain coming down in silvery sheets. She was too angry to be heartbroken. It was all so clear now. The date Monday night didn't count. It had been a simple dinner date prompted by a newly discovered mutual interest. But then she'd started talking, so he'd asked her out again. And Tuesday night she had really given him an earful, so how about Wednesday? Then Friday. His bonus had been an enthusiastic tumble in bed.

God, she was an idiot! From the minute he'd

gazed deeply into her eyes she had conveniently
forgotten everything she'd ever heard about him.
How willingly she had devoured all that garbage
about strewing rose petals and lilacs at her feet.
A sixteen-year-old wouldn't have swallowed that.

Lori leaned her head against the jamb and let a
few tears splash out of her eyes and down her
cheeks. *Well, Mom,* she thought. *How's this?
Rash and impulsive enough for you?*

AT THAT MOMENT Luke was turning the pickup
into the driveway of the Priest house. He jumped
out of the vehicle and ran through the rain to the
front door. Mary Alice answered his ring, and
when she saw him, the look on her face was one
of pure delight. ''Luke! I thought Brock wanted
you to work today.''

''What in hell can you do in this kind of
weather? I've got news, real news, and it couldn't
wait.''

''Oh, this is so grand!'' Mary Alice gushed.
''Come in.'' She led the way into the living room.

''Where's your mama?'' Luke asked.

''Playing cards down the street. She won't be
home for at least an hour.'' Mary Alice turned,
slipped her arms around Luke's neck and kissed

him soundly. Then she pulled him down on the sofa with her.

"It's finally going to happen, sugar," he said. "The big day is upon us."

"Luke!"

"That old rancher in Fort Worth, Mr. Wiggins, called me about an hour ago. He's ready to sell, so I'll be going to the bank in Fredericksburg this week and withdrawing my money. Then next Saturday, I'm supposed to drive up there and clinch the deal."

Mary Alice closed her eyes and held her hands to her chest. It was finally going to happen! She had reached her personal pot at the end of the rainbow at last! "Oh, Luke, I'm so excited!"

"Yeah, so am I. I've waited a long time for this. A long time. Ever since Wyoming."

Mary Alice could hardly contain herself. "Nothing can happen now, can it?"

"Not unless the old bastard gets stubborn about the five hundred."

"What five hundred?"

"He wants five hundred more than I've got, but I'm hoping when he sees a cashier's check for the rest, he'll take the money and just forget about the piddlin' five hundred."

"Well, if he won't, I've got five hundred." She clapped her hands together with glee.

Luke favored her with his warmest smile, the one that had worked like a charm for him on so many occasions. "That's sweet, Mary Alice, real sweet. I won't use it unless I absolutely have to."

Mary Alice jumped to her feet. "Let me write you a check now. That way you'll have the money if you need it. If you don't, you can just tear up the check."

Luke rubbed his chin. "Well, that might be a good idea. Like I said, I won't use it unless he gets really stubborn."

Mary Alice took her checkbook out of her handbag, wrote the check and handed it to him. He folded it and put it in his pocket. "I really do thank you, sugar."

"It's only money," she said with a little laugh. She would have given Luke anything she owned. Still, she experienced a twinge or two when she wrote the amount in the check register and saw her bank balance after the five hundred had been deducted. That little nest egg had been her security blanket for a long time. But the ranch, *their* ranch was worth it. "How long will you have to be in Fort Worth?"

"I'm not sure. The ranch is about twenty miles

west of the city. I don't know if there are any business details to be worked out."

"Won't you have to work next Saturday?"

"Naw, I'll get out of it."

"Now, Luke…now do we know when we'll be leaving?"

He pursed his lips. "The day after New Year's. Plan on that."

"Can I tell them at work?"

"Nope. I don't want it getting around."

Mary Alice's face clouded. "But I…I can't just not show up for work one morning. It isn't right."

"I told you—you don't owe 'em a thing. Your mama hasn't been talking at the beauty shop, has she?"

She glanced down at her hands, then up again. "No, because I asked her not to, but she just feels awful about doing that to Vera Madison. Vera didn't really need a full-time manicurist, but she let Mama stay on."

"All that's behind her now," Luke said, growing impatient with the conversation.

"Gee, it's so hard to believe it's actually going to happen."

"I know, but that's next weekend. What about now?"

"I'm making chili. You'll stay and eat, won't you?"

"Sure. Can't pass up homemade chili. Want to go to a movie or something afterward?"

"That might be fun if there's something on we haven't seen. Or we could rent a video."

"Whatever."

"Oh, this is so wonderful! Want me to get you a beer?"

"That'd be nice, sugar."

"Be right back." But before going to the kitchen, Mary Alice walked to a window, pushed back the curtain and peered out. "Luke, I don't think we'd better plan on going anywhere, and you might have to sleep on the sofa tonight. The radio says we're under a flash flood warning. Would you mind?"

"Not a bit, if it's okay with your mama."

"Mama won't care. I'll go get that beer."

Luke settled against the back of the sofa and propped his feet on the coffee table, sighing a sigh of the utmost contentment. Now he could forget all the rotten years—Rawlins, the sojourns through Colorado, New Mexico and half of Texas, wondering how the hell he was going to find the goose that would lay his golden egg. It was about time things finally started going his way. There was a lucky star in the heavens, and it had his name on it.

CHAPTER TEN

CODY HAD BEEN GONE less than ten minutes when there was a heavy pounding on Lori's door. She rushed to open it and found him standing on the stoop, looking furious and sheepish all at the same time. And very, very wet.

"I can't go home," he growled. "The barricades are up. The road's under water."

He shrugged out of his jacket and gave it a good shake before entering the house. "I'm going to drip all over your carpet."

"I can sop it up. Obviously, you're going to have to get out of those clothes. I have a washer and dryer."

"And what do you suggest I wear?"

"I don't know. I'll find something."

What she found was an ancient flannel bathrobe that was roomy on her but stretched tightly across Cody's shoulders and came to just below his knees. He looked utterly ridiculous in it, but neither of them was inclined to laugh.

"I'll put your clothes in the washer," she said, turning and heading for the bathroom where the appliances were.

Cody watched as she dumped the clothes in the washer and turned it on. Her movements were quick and jerky. "Are you really angry?" he asked.

Lori closed the washer lid, then turned to him, crossing her arms under her breasts. "I think disappointed is a better word."

Cody opened his mouth to say something, then closed it and sighed wearily. A second or two passed before he said, "Then that's your problem, not mine." Scowling, he sat on the sofa, picked up a two-day-old newspaper and began turning the pages.

Lori endured the silence a few minutes. If this wasn't something! How were they supposed to get through the rest of the day? By sniping and snarling at each other? "I guess we should try to be civil," she said. "These are pretty close quarters, and fate seems to have thrust us together in them."

"I'll do my best," Cody replied not looking up.

As rapidly as he was turning the pages of the paper, Lori knew he couldn't possibly be reading anything. She went to the kitchen and began needlessly scrubbing the sink. "Help yourself to TV or music or whatever."

"Thanks." He didn't move.

"Would you like me to make coffee?"

"Not for me, thanks."

More silence. Lori rolled her eyes toward the ceiling. "If this is your best, then you're lousy company."

The paper came crashing down. "What in hell do you expect?"

"You have to admit it seems rather pat...the big rush all of a sudden," she insisted stubbornly.

"I admit nothing of the kind. Were you or were you not dating someone until recently?"

"Well, I..."

Cody got to his feet, crossed the room and stood in front of her. "This has got to stop. I'm sorry you've spent even a minute doubting my motives and words where you are concerned. I wish none of the trouble at the bank had a thing to do with a friend of yours. But I can't let personal feelings intimidate me into not doing my job. Surely you can understand that."

He waited for her to say something. When she didn't, he went on.

"I'm asking you to believe I never lied to you or used you or did any of the nefarious things you've accused me of. I never pumped you for information, did I?''

''I...I don't remember.''

''I never spent five minutes with you for any reason other than simply wanting to be with you. I knew at the book fair I was going to ask you out if the coach was no longer around. I knew at Cooper's I was going to ask you out again, and that was before you said a word about Mary Alice. And at the country club dance I knew I was going to ask you out again and again and again. And at the McKinneys I knew we were going to sleep together, probably sooner instead of later. I just knew.''

Lori knew she should be careful because she wanted to believe him. But she could feel her resolve crumbling. ''Well, I...''

''Don't let me go off to Houston this week with things not right between us.'' He brushed her cheek with the back of his hand. ''I haven't felt like I was falling in love since I was seventeen. Please don't spoil it for me. Let me enjoy it.''

Lori closed her eyes....

THE RAIN STOPPED during the night, and the sun came out Monday morning. Lori lay very still with her face pressed against Cody's back, one arm under her pillow, the other thrown across his stomach. How she hated it that the weekend was drawing to a close, especially since he was going to be gone until Friday. She took a selfish minute to wish the road wouldn't open, but with the sun out it would and very quickly.

She felt him stir. "What time is it?" he asked sleepily.

"Seven-thirty."

"I don't hear any rain."

"No, it's stopped, and the sun's coming out."

"Guess I don't have an excuse not to go to Houston."

"You don't enjoy the meetings of the great minds?"

"They're a pain in the ass." Turning, he gathered her into his arms. "I'm going to miss you. You've brought some badly needed joy into my life."

"That's nice to hear." Lori knew she should be happier than she'd ever been in her life…and to a certain extent she was. Oh, she was still worried about Mary Alice but totally confident that she didn't take the money. And if she didn't, no one could prove she did, could they?

So Lori knew Mary Alice wasn't responsible for her uneasy feeling. She wished Cody would open up and talk to her about…oh, about his childhood, his hopes and dreams for the future, something deep and personal so she could get inside his head.

"How long before the road opens, do you think?" he asked.

"Give it an hour or so. Once the rain stops, it doesn't take long. I'll put the coffee on."

Later, after Cody had dressed, he phoned his office and explained to Martha that he'd got caught out of town and had had to wait for the water to recede. He then asked if anything or anyone needed his attention. Lori heard him say, "Well, tell Helen Merriwether to fill in during peak periods. I'll have to go home and change clothes before coming in, but with luck, I'll be there before noon. Thanks, Martha. Goodbye."

Hanging up, he glanced over at Lori. "Mary Alice called in sick this morning."

"So? Does that further implicate her?"

"Goddammit, Lori," he barked, then checked himself. "It was nothing but an idle comment. Don't be so touchy where she's concerned."

They had breakfast, then Cody got ready to leave. "Are you going to the bank this morning?" he asked Lori.

"I don't think so. "

"Then I won't see you until Friday...unless the road's still closed. If so, I'll be right back."

"I know another way to town...higher ground."

A flicker of amusement crossed his face. "Why didn't you tell me that yesterday?"

"I can't imagine."

He kissed her goodbye with such deliberate sensuality it stripped her of her senses. "Remember *that* this week," he said when he lifted his head, "and forget all that other garbage. I'll try to call you this week."

Then he was gone, leaving Lori with the most peculiar feeling of loss.

"CYNTHIA, I mean this from my heart," Lori said as she leaned over the crib. "Jennifer is a beautiful baby. I mean not just cute. She's beautiful."

Cynthia, of course, beamed. "Naturally we all think so. She's a good baby, too...so far. I hope she doesn't turn out spoiled rotten. One peep out of that tiny mouth, and Virginia and Lettie Mae come running. I've told them Jennifer *needs* to cry sometimes."

Giving the baby another gentle pat, Lori straightened. "How are you?"

"Great. Never felt better in my life. I'm glad you stopped by, Lori. How about a cup of tea?"

"I'd love one."

"Good. No one else in this house drinks the stuff except in iced form."

The two women left the nursery and went downstairs, Cynthia leading the way to the sun room. "Have a seat," she said. "I'll be right back."

Lori sat in one of the wicker chairs and gazed out over the grounds of the Double C. It was Thursday afternoon. The week had found her staying close to her house and her work. She'd gone to the bank Tuesday morning and done some Christmas shopping, but that was the only time she'd been away from the ranch. Finally today she'd felt a bad case of cabin fever setting in, so she'd decided to visit Cynthia and Jennifer. Cody had called from Houston every night, but he wouldn't be calling tonight because of the retirement party—a stag affair that he feared might last until the wee hours. He claimed to be bored to death and missing her terribly. She hoped that was true.

Cynthia returned shortly carrying a tray that held two cups and saucers and a teapot. The glass-topped table in the center of the room was strewn with newspapers. She pushed them aside and set down the tray. As she poured tea for Lori, she indicated one of the papers. "I've been reading about Cody's father," she said casually, handing Lori a cup.

"Cody's father?" Lori asked, puzzled.

"Uh-huh. J.T. always gets the Sunday edition of the Houston *Post* along with the Austin paper. To show you how busy a baby can keep you, I'm just now getting around to reading it. And I always devour the business section. Cody's father is obviously a very big shot in the city. Here, read it yourself."

Lori was sure there had been some mistake, but she took the paper and began reading.

DeWitt Hendricks, CEO of the huge Southwest Bank conglomerate, is spearheading a task force aimed at securing a big slice of the lucrative Mexican free-trade market for Houston. "We musn't flag in our efforts," Hendricks said, "because Dallas and San Antonio are breathing down our necks." He also indicated that his sons, Robert and Cody, would be utilized when necessary, and hinted that he wouldn't hesitate to invest some of his own one-hundred-million dollar fortune in the Mexican venture.

The article was a lengthy one, but Lori had read enough. With a great deal of effort, she kept a straight face as she glanced up at Cynthia. She even managed a smile.

"Impressive?" Cynthia asked.

"Yes, it's...very interesting." Lori took a sip of tea and almost gagged on it. "Have you finished with the paper, Cynthia? I'd like to read the entire article when I have the time."

"Sure, take it. Oh, isn't it nice to have all that rain gone? Are you looking forward to Christmas, Lori? Where will you spend it? In San Antonio?"

"I'm sure I will."

"Are you taking Cody with you?"

Lori's eyes clouded. "I certainly doubt that."

IT WASN'T until midway through Thursday night's retirement party that Cody decided *how* he would find out who took the money. His solution was ludicrous, of course, but once the idea took hold of him, it wouldn't let go. That night, lying in the quiet dark of the River Oaks mansion, in the bedroom that had been his since childhood, he discarded the notion half a dozen times, only to pick it up again. Yes, it was what he was going to do, he finally decided firmly. And somehow he thought Lori would approve.

The following morning he left Houston at sunrise, pausing only long enough to leave his parents a note. At an all-night diner he bought coffee and a doughnut for the road. When he arrived back in Crystal Creek, he went home to change, but then he didn't go directly to the bank. Instead, he drove to the Double C Ranch. Some people would think him crazy, he knew, but he felt Lori would understand why he was standing on the front porch of the McKinney residence, punching the doorbell.

Virginia Parks answered the ring. "Why, good morning, Mr. Hendricks."

"Good morning, Ms. Parks."

"I'm Virginia," the housekeeper said.

"And I'm Cody."

"Come in, Cody. I believe J.T. is in his study."

Cody stepped into the foyer. "I...ah, didn't come to see J.T. this morning, Virginia. Actually, I'd like to talk to Hank, if that's all right."

Virginia's expression conveyed mild surprise. "Hank? Of course it's all right. He loves company and doesn't get near enough of it these days. I believe he's in the sun room. It's the warmest room in the house in the morning. Gets the east sun, you know. This way.''

Cody followed the housekeeper. ''I promise I won't keep him but a few minutes.''

Virginia glanced over her shoulder and smiled. ''You'll keep him as long as he wants to be kept.''

Hank was sitting in a wicker rocker facing the big windows. A sweater had been thrown around his shoulders, and his cane was hooked over the arm of the rocker. He seemed to be staring vacantly out over the vista of the ranch. He looked very bent and old, but the minute Virginia entered the room, he straightened, and his eyes grew alert.

''You have a visitor, Hank,'' Virginia announced, then turned and walked away.

Hank peered through his wire-rimmed glasses, apparently confused for a minute...but only for a minute. ''Ah, you're Lori's young feller, ain'tcha?''

''Yes, sir.''

''I told you not to call me sir. Know somethin'...you look like a banker.''

''Should I thank you for the compliment?''

''Not specially. You fellers always look like you're on the way to a funeral.''

Cody chuckled. He removed his coat, loosened

his tie and rolled his shirtsleeves to his elbows. "That better?"

"Much. Sit down, take the load off'a your feet and tell me what'cha want to see me about. Guess it's about all that oil I was tellin' you about."

Cody carefully laid his coat across the back of a chair and sat down. "Actually, Hank, I *have* been thinking about that, but it requires more study than I've been able to give it in just a few days. What I really came here about this morning is..."

Cody couldn't believe he was really doing this, and if his father or brother had gotten wind of it, he probably would have been committed to an institution for the mentally unbalanced. *I guess my problem is,* he thought, *that I don't think like a banker.*

"You see, Hank...last weekend, Lori told me something about the visions you have."

"Been havin' 'em all my life. Lotsa folks think I'm purely crazy...not that I give a good goddamn what lotsa folks think."

"She said you had 'seen' someone steal something from Carolyn."

"Yep."

"I'm very curious about your visions. Do they

just come to you unbidden, or do they involve things you've been thinking about for a while?''

Hank scratched his stubbled chin. ''Little o' both, I reckon. Like the oil. I'd been thinkin' about that property for a spell. But the bi'ness about someone stealin' from Carolyn—that jus' popped into my head out'a the blue. Don't rightly know what it was that was stolen, but they must'a got to the bottom of it 'cause I ain't heard a word about it.''

''When did you see that, Hank?''

''Oh, a few weeks back. It was on a Sunday night, I remember that much.''

Cody felt his heartbeat quicken. ''Did…did you see who did the stealing?''

''Nope. I jus' knew somethin' was missin'.'' Hank peered at Cody quizzically. ''What's this all about, young feller?''

Leaning forward, Cody lowered his voice and spoke earnestly. ''Hank, there's something I'd like to tell you, something that isn't common knowledge, and I'd appreciate it if you'd keep it under your hat.''

''Ain't a soul alive who's better at keepin' a secret than yours truly.''

''Thanks. You see, there's some money missing

from the bank, and you're right, it was taken from one of Carolyn's accounts.''

A look of pure triumph crossed Hank's wizened face, but he said nothing.

''It's not a great deal of money,'' Cody went on, ''so I squared it with Carolyn, passing it off as a bookkeeping error. But the money's not been recovered. Obviously, someone at the bank took it, and I want to know who it was. And I'd like to find out myself, rather than have some auditor do it for me...if you get my drift.''

Hank nodded knowingly. ''I got'cha.''

''So I was wondering...if you thought about it, concentrated on it real hard, do you think you might come up with something for me?''

Hank stared at him a minute, then smiled. ''Know somethin'...I ain't met three bankers in my whole life I liked, but I like you.''

''Well, thank you. I'm very flattered.''

''And I'm gonna see what I can do for you. I'll think and ponder on it a spell. Can't never tell what I might come up with.''

Cody stood. ''I'd appreciate that, Hank. More than I can tell you.''

''Don't mention it. Any banker who believes is all right in my book.''

Cody rolled down his sleeves, straightened his

tie and reached for his coat. "Is it all right if I call in a few days?"

Hank nodded. "I'll be here. Understand...I can't guarantee nothin'."

"I understand. Thank you."

A minute later when Cody stepped out into the autumn sunshine and headed for his car, he began whistling. He knew he should feel like the world's biggest ass, but he didn't. Instead he felt as though he might finally be on the verge of finding out what happened to that confounded money.

At the gate he automatically turned toward town, but a few miles down the road, he braked and made a U-turn. No one was expecting him at any particular time. He had given Martha a vague "I'll be back sometime Friday," so she would expect him when she saw him. It was a beautiful day, and he felt curiously unburdened. And he had missed Lori horribly. He drove straight for the Circle T, alive with longing and imagining the loving reception waiting for him.

Lori answered his knock. She was wearing jeans, a floppy shirt and sneakers. Her hair had been carelessly twisted atop her head, and she wore no makeup. To his eyes she looked all of twenty—fresh and incredibly beautiful. He fully expected her to fling herself into his arms.

Instead, her face became as cold and hard as marble. "What are you doing, slumming?" She turned away and moved to the center of the room.

"What?" Perplexed, Cody stepped inside and closed the door. Walking to her, he slipped his arms around her waist and kissed the top of her head. "I thought of almost nothing but you all week."

"Really? You must not have contributed much to the meeting of the great minds."

Cody felt a sudden chill. "What's the matter with you?"

Lori took his hands and flung them away from her, then walked to the coffee table and picked up a newspaper. Cody couldn't begin to imagine what was wrong. When he'd talked to her Wednesday night, she had been so sweet, breathlessly telling him how much she wanted to see him.

But then she thrust the newspaper against his chest, and he knew. He didn't even have to look at the paper to know. When his brother had proudly shown the article to him, his first reaction had been to pray no one in Crystal Creek had seen it. But then he'd reminded himself that the locals did not read the Post. The Austin and San Antonio papers, yes, but he'd never seen so much as one copy of the Post in Crystal Creek.

"Where did you get this?" he asked.

She uttered an unpleasant sound. "The McKinneys get the Sunday edition, and Cynthia, the banker, reads the business section. She could hardly wait to show it to me."

"Jesus!" Resignedly, he tossed the paper in the nearest chair.

"Just what is behind this masquerading as a small-town banker? Are you getting a kick out of living and working among the hicks? You could buy and sell this entire town if you took a notion to."

"No, I couldn't."

"Then your daddy could."

"Am I supposed to apologize? So my family has money. They had money before I was born, and I had no say about who my parents were."

"You've misrepresented yourself, Cody, and you know it."

"Okay, okay. I'll admit I would prefer that the local citizens don't know who my father is."

"Why?"

"Because it would set me apart. The people at the bank wouldn't take me seriously if they knew my father is CEO of Southwest Bank. I'd rather they think I got where I am because I know my job and do it well, nothing else. I really don't understand what difference it makes who or what my father is, but unfortunately, it always seems to."

Lori heaved a sigh. That article had alarmed her in ways she didn't fully comprehend. She'd read it so many times she had the damned thing memorized. His family wasn't just rich; they were Big Rich, the elite. And the money had been around a few generations. Old money in Texas was powerful. The article had stressed the power. DeWitt Hendricks, it said, had only to pick up a telephone and have the ear of congressmen, senators, cabinet members and even the President. He had the kind of clout that ordinary people couldn't imagine.

Lori had known of families like Cody's—San Antonio had its share—and they tended to stay with their own kind. Dalliances with waitresses, secretaries and, yes, accountants were not frowned upon provided they remained only dalliances. And that frightened her. She was in deep emotionally and not sure she could extricate herself gracefully.

"You and I do not inhabit the same world," she said.

"See!" Cody shouted, jabbing a finger in the air. "See! That's exactly the kind of thinking that prompted me to clam up about my family. It's the most preposterous thing I've ever heard, and I've run up against it too many times to count. But I'm surprised at you, Lori. I wouldn't have thought that you, of all people, would give such a thing a thought."

"Then why didn't you tell me about your family straight away?"

He opened his mouth, then shut it, fuming.

"I think you're getting a kick out of seeing how the common folks live. For sure I don't think a small town accountant would..." Lori checked herself.

"Would what?"

"Nothing."

Cody simply stared at her a minute, stunned by what was happening. Then he threw up his hands. "You're a snob!"

A minute of uncomfortable silence passed. Then Lori's shoulders rose and fell. "I think I'm a realist. You're just having a good time and will be gone when this fling with small-town life palls. It was, unfortunately, more than that for me."

Cody stared at her bowed head, and a slow smile crossed his face. Closing the space between them, he took her in his arms. Though she didn't exactly respond, she didn't push him away. "This is too ridiculous to talk about. Okay, you want to know about my family. I'll tell you all about them. Then I'll tell you what I came to tell you in the first place. But can we please sit down?"

SOMETIME LATER, after Cody had finished talking, Lori sighed and shook her head. "I always knew there was something about yourself you weren't telling me. I couldn't imagine what it was. I *never* would have imagined that."

"It was that life that brought me to Crystal Creek. And I've loved it here. You can't imagine how free I've felt. But you're right—it won't last. The day will come when I'll have to go back to Houston and take my 'rightful place.' I owe it to the family. I realized it this past week. Someday my father will retire, Robert will become CEO and I'll take over the flagship. There's no escaping it, and for all the differences Dad and I have had in the past, I don't want to escape my heritage."

"Well, I'll never be able to say I wasn't warned."

"Lori…" His voice was low and husky, and he trained those fascinating eyes on her. "I wouldn't hesitate to take you with me if that's what we want at the time. My family can be so staid and stuffy at times. You'd inject some sparkle into that house. Now, will you kiss me hello?''

She leaned toward him, and he drew her into his arms. He kissed her mouth, her cheek, her throat and ear before releasing her. She sat back, smiling. ''Cody, what did you want to tell me?''

''Huh?''

''You said you came here to tell me something.''

''Oh, yeah. I came to tell you I've hit on a way to solve the mystery of the missing two thousand, and it won't involve using anything you told me about Mary Alice and Luke. It won't involve any more snooping. In fact, I'll stay out of it entirely. And…I think, I hope it's almost foolproof.''

Interest flickered in Lori's eyes. ''What are you going to do?''

''I've…ah, put Hank on the case.''

Lori's eyes widened. *''What?''*

''You heard me. He knew the theft had occurred before anyone else did. Now he's going to try to come up with who did it. He says he can sometimes do that if he ponders on things a bit.'' He couldn't bring himself to look at her. As he said it aloud, it sounded even more ridiculous than it had while he'd mulled it over last night. But he was counting on her to understand. There was a single gasp of astonishment. "Cody! Being a believer is one thing, but this?"

Cody was all seriousness. "I knew I had to do something, Lori."

"B-but, Cody, there's no guarantee that Hank will come up with anything."

"I'm aware of that."

"If he doesn't, what are you going to do?"

He hesitated...but only for a second. "I'll call Audit."

"But you didn't want to do that. You said you could get in trouble."

"I'm not going to get 'in trouble.' I might get called on the carpet for handing the money over to Carolyn so readily, but I'll get over it."

"Your father won't be impressed."

"I know, but I'll do anything I have to. I want to divorce myself from...whatever happens. That way I can concentrate on us." He took one of her curls and twisted it around his finger. "I've been away from you much too long, and there's really no urgency about getting to the office."

Without a word, she took him by the hand and led him to the bedroom. There was another long, lovely weekend ahead.

CHAPTER ELEVEN

MARY ALICE WAS CERTAIN Saturday was the longest day of her life. She cleaned house from top to bottom, but she was constantly on the alert for the telephone's ring. Luke had told her he was leaving for Fort Worth early that morning and would get in touch with her as soon as he had news, but she hadn't expected to have to wait so long. It was unbearable.

The waiting finally stopped at five o'clock. "Hi, sugar," Luke said when she answered the phone. "Well, the deed's done. I'm now the proud owner of two hundred acres of the Grand Prairie. That's what they call this area up here, and I'm sure hoping it's gonna be grand for me."

"Oh, Luke! I'm so relieved to hear from you."

"Listen, sugar. Old Man Wiggins wouldn't budge a penny on the price. I'm afraid I had to use your five hundred."

"Th-that's okay. Are you coming home tonight?"

"Nope. Wiggins and I are going into town to sorta celebrate. I'm gonna stay here in his house tonight. And he says there's some folks he wants me to meet, people who can help me get started."

"Oh, well..." Mary Alice fought her disappointment. "Tomorrow then. What time?"

"I'm not sure. Depends on what all has to be worked out. But as soon as I get back, I'll call."

"All right, Luke."

"Wiggins is waiting for me, so gotta run. You take care."

"You, too. Goodbye. Luke, I love you."

But he had already hung up. Replacing the receiver, Mary Alice experienced a strange sort of twinge. She had expected to be absolutely elated when this finally happened, but instead she felt... funny.

Then it dawned on her why. She had no idea where Luke was. She had no phone number, no way of reaching him. He was about twenty miles outside Fort Worth, but in what direction? She supposed that shouldn't worry her, but it did. In fact, she felt close to panic.

Why hadn't she thought of this before?

"THIS IS SO WONDERFUL," Lori cooed, eyes shining as she laid her cheek on Cody's bare chest.

"Yes, it is," he agreed, stroking her curls.

"My, God, Cody, it's Sunday morning!"

"So?"

"I don't think we've been out of this bed except to eat since Friday night."

"Do you have a problem with that?"

Smiling, she ran the tip of her tongue over his flat brown nipple. "Not a bit. You and I might really be able to pull off the sixteen-day bit. I certainly feel properly mated right now." Sitting up, she reached for his blue robe. The bed covers, she noticed, were a tangled mess. She shrugged into the robe, cinched its belt around her waist and tucked the garment beneath her.

"Don't tell me...you're hungry."

"How'd you guess?" Fortunately, the larder was well stocked. Lori had seen to that Friday. They had driven into his garage around six o'clock Friday evening after a stop at the supermarket, and from that moment on, they had shut the rest of the world out.

More important, they hadn't whispered the names Mary Alice Priest and Luke Harte. Lori had finally convinced herself that Mary Alice's problems were not hers. She wasn't even going to think about them but concentrate on Cody instead.

"Do you still insist on going home this afternoon?" Cody asked.

"I think so. We both have work tomorrow. Plus I haven't done any housework or laundry in… days and days. We can't carry on half the night the way we've been doing."

"Too bad. I like having you here in my house."

"That pleases me."

Lori liked Cody's house. It was located in a section of town where those who "had made it" bought homes. All of them were well kept and nicely landscaped. The decor in Cody's was masculine without being cold, and it was so perfectly done she suspected an interior decorator had been employed. Yet the house looked lived in, as though he really enjoyed it, that it wasn't just a place to sleep and change clothes.

"There's no hurry about getting home. Not until after lunch," she said, patting his bare chest. "Now I'm going to make coffee and fix breakfast."

LATER, THEY DECIDED to get out of the house and enjoy a sunny autumn day. They drove to Llano for barbecue again before he dropped her off at her place. Then on the way home, Cody passed the Double C. He stopped, hesitated, then drove through the gate.

Cynthia answered his ring.

"Why, hello, Cody. It's nice to see you again."

"Thanks. I'm not intruding, I hope."

"Of course not. Come in."

"How are you and the baby?" he asked as he stepped into the foyer.

"We're both splendid, thanks. By the way, I read that article about your father in last Sunday's *Post*."

"I...ah, know. Lori told me."

"If you think about it, ask him if he knows Joseph Page from Boston. He's my father. All my male relatives are bankers."

"Joseph Page. I'll try to remember that."

"Did you want to see J.T.?"

"No. I wonder if I might speak to Hank a minute."

"Hank? Well, of course. He's in the sun room. It's right this way."

"I know where it is, Cynthia. Thanks."

The old man was in his customary spot. "Good afternoon, Hank," Cody said.

"Hello, young feller. I was just thinkin' about you."

"Oh?"

"I've been doin' some powerful ponderin' since I talked to you, and I had me a dream last night."

Cody's heartbeat quickened. Lord, he hoped this would be what he needed. Life was very sweet and satisfying right now. The only sour note in it was the theft. "I hope you have some news for me."

"Maybe. A woman took that money."

"Did...did you see her face?"

"Nope. Didn't see the face of the feller she gave it to, either."

"She...gave the money to a man?"

"Yep. Saw it plain as day. He 'peared to be a cowboy. He wore one of them hats, y'know. Oh, and he had face fuzz—a mustache."

Hank's absolutely amazing, Cody thought, *but I have nothing...nothing.* A hundred-year-old man "saw" a woman give Carolyn's money to a mustached cowboy, and though Cody's hunches were working overtime, he knew nothing certain. That meant only one thing: in the morning he was going to have to call Houston and request an audit. He couldn't remember ever hating anything more.

The minute he got home he called Lori. "I talked to Hank," he said.

"What did he say?"

"That a woman took the money and gave it to a cowboy with a mustache."

He heard her suck in her breath. "But...that doesn't mean it was Mary Alice and Luke."

"No, it doesn't. You're sure right about that."

But for the first time Cody heard something different in her voice—doubt. Now Lori doubted, too. *God, please give me a break in this thing.*

THE FOLLOWING MORNING, Mary Alice slipped into her cage, her face a picture of worry. At the next station, Gina Otis looked at her with concern. "Are you sick, Mary Alice?"

"Sick?"

"That's the third time you've been to the rest room since you came to work."

"Oh...just a little stomach upset."

"Do you have something to take for it?"

"Yes...yes. Thanks, Gina."

Mary Alice's stomach was in a knot, but illness had nothing to do with that. She had been down to the rest room area three times, all right, but only because it was where the pay phones were. She had called the bunkhouse twice and gotten no answer. Finally she had tried Brock Munroe's house. "No, Mary Alice," Brock had said, "I haven't seen him this morning. He asked for the weekend off. No problem since we don't do a thing around here from Friday till Monday, but I expected him here this morning. I don't have any idea where he is.''

Mary Alice had never been so nervous in her life. Sunday had been terrible, much worse than Saturday. She hadn't left the house for fear Luke would call or come by, but she hadn't heard a word from him, not a word. How could he do this to her? The least he could do was call.

Maybe he'd had car trouble on the way back from Fort Worth. That old truck wasn't very reliable. But even if he was broken down somewhere, wouldn't he call so she wouldn't worry? Sadly she decided he might not. In some ways, Luke wasn't the most thoughtful or considerate person she had ever known.

We don't do a thing around here from Friday till Monday. Brock's words came back to her. But Luke had to work every Friday night. She just didn't understand.

A customer appeared at the window wanting to cash a check. Mary Alice's hands were trembling so badly she could hardly count out the bills. Then a steady stream of people followed, so she forced herself to concentrate on the business at hand.

Finally there was a lull, and her personal worries assailed her again. Where in the world Luke was wasn't the only thing troubling her. She felt just terrible about leaving the bank without giving notice, and her conscience was giving her a fit. Mr. Hendricks was the nicest person in the world to work for; it wasn't fair to him.

Besides, if she simply didn't return to work after the holidays, she couldn't expect a good reference from him. In spite of what Luke said, she suspected their financial situation would demand that she work, at least for the first couple of years. She needed a good reference, and the bank was the only place she'd ever worked. Luke was terribly sure of himself, certain they would get along just fine without a paycheck from her, but she was beginning to realize there was a great deal of "pie in the sky" to Luke's way of thinking.

However, she and her mother could write a book on making do and doing without. She liked to prepare for the unexpected.

Mary Alice's loyalty to Luke warred with her conscience, and the conscience won. Putting the Next Window Please sign in place, she explained to Gina that she needed to speak to Mr. Hendricks, then hurried up the steps to the mezzanine.

Cody was just on the point of calling Houston

about an audit when the buzzer on his intercom sounded. "Yes, Martha?"

"Mary Alice Priest is here, Mr. Hendricks. She would like to speak to you if you have a minute."

"Of course. Send her in." Cody couldn't recall that Mary Alice had ever before come upstairs and asked to speak to him. He got to his feet as the door opened.

"Good morning, Mary Alice. Please come in and have a seat."

The young woman timidly crossed the room and sat in one of the chairs facing his desk. Cody thought he had never seen anyone look more terrified. Her eyes were wide, and she was clutching her hands so hard her knuckles were white. His own heart began to race as he wondered what she would say—perhaps a confession—but outwardly he appeared cool and calm. He took his seat and gave her what he hoped was a reassuring smile. "You wanted to speak with me?"

She cleared her throat. "Yes, sir. I'm sorry I've waited so long to tell you this, Mr. Hendricks, but I won't be returning to work after New Year's."

"Oh?" Cody's instincts shifted into high gear. "Isn't this rather sudden?"

"Y-yes. Well, yes and no. I've…suspected for some time I might have to leave, but I didn't find

out for sure until recently. I...really am sorry. I
hope I haven't put you in a bind. I could start
training someone right away, and if I don't finish
by the time I leave...well, one of the other tellers
could take over. I really am sorry.''

"Have you been unhappy working here?''

''Oh, no! Oh, goodness, I've just loved working here, Mr. Hendricks. This bank is...well, it's
like a second home to me, and it's been nothing
short of a godsend for Mama and me. If I was
staying in Crystal Creek, I guess I'd work for
Southwest forever.''

''You're leaving town?''

''Yes, Mama and I are moving away.''

Cody thought of what he knew about Mary Alice, both the dry data in her personnel file and the
things Lori had told him. The young woman and
her mother lived together and had a tough time
getting by financially. Both of them had lived in
Crystal Creek all their lives. They owned a home
here. What would make them leave? Better jobs?
Somehow he didn't think so. Experienced bank
tellers and manicurists could usually find work
anywhere, but they probably did better money-
wise by staying put. Mary Alice had acquired
some seniority at the bank, and her mother doubtless had a loyal clientele.

"Have you accepted a job elsewhere?" Cody knew perfectly well it was none of his business, but he hoped Mary Alice would keep talking. Maybe he was way off base, but he couldn't shake the notion that her leaving had something to do with the theft. If so, Luke Harte had to be involved.

"No, sir, I... Well, I'm really not supposed to tell anyone this, so I'd appreciate it if you wouldn't say anything, but...I'm getting married."

"Married? That's...wonderful, Mary Alice. Congratulations."

"Thanks." She smiled for the first time since coming into the office. "My boyfriend isn't ready for that to get around, so..."

"Why?" Again Cody knew he was asking a question he had no right to ask.

"I...don't know, sir, but he's very adamant about it."

"Well, rest assured I won't tell anyone. Is the young man in question anyone I would know?"

"I'm not sure. His name is Luke Harte."

"I've met him. He's a very lucky man."

"Thanks." Mary Alice blushed. "I'll be happy to work overtime training someone. I really do feel terrible about giving you such short notice."

"We'll see." Cody smiled. "It could be there's someone on the waiting list who has experience."

"I hope so." Mary Alice stood and smoothed at her skirt with the palms of her hands. "I guess that's all. I really do thank you for being so nice about this."

Cody got to his feet. "Don't mention it. I wish you all the luck in the world, Mary Alice."

"Thank you." She stood uncertainly in front of him for a second or two, then turned and left the office. Her heart was pounding like crazy. She could only pray Luke never found out she had given Mr. Hendricks notice. Though he'd never been angry with her, she had a feeling an angry Luke would be hard to reckon with.

Returning to her station, she removed the sign. "Gina, has anyone mentioned there being a call for me?"

"No. Not to me, at least."

Mary Alice asked the same question of the other tellers, but no one had heard anything about a call for her. Sighing, she wondered if she should try phoning the bunkhouse again. Where was Luke? She was beginning to worry that something awful might have happened to him.

UPSTAIRS, Cody paced his office a few minutes before reaching for the phone and dialing Lori's number. He let it ring five times before hanging up. Glancing at his watch, he saw it was almost ten. She'd told him she had to come to the bank this morning, so she was probably on the way. He hurried downstairs, satisfied himself that she wasn't there, then went to Helen Merriwether's desk.

"Helen, you know Lori Porter, right?"

"Of course."

"Good. I want you to fasten your eyes on that front door, and the minute Lori walks through it, pounce on her. I have to see her upstairs pronto. Got that?"

"Sure, Mr. Hendricks. Of course."

Returning to his office, Cody told Martha he was expecting Mrs. Porter, then sat behind his desk and waited. It was only ten minutes but it seemed like forever before there was a tap on his door and Lori entered.

He wondered how long he would have to be around her before the mere sight of her stopped doing peculiar things to his equilibrium. This morning she was wearing a dress in a bright shade of blue. With her dark hair and smooth, creamy complexion she could wear any color, but she looked especially great in vibrant ones.

"Good morning," he said, coming out from behind the desk. "You're the most gorgeous thing I've ever seen."

"I know you didn't tell Helen to send me up here pronto so you could tell me that."

"Well, I don't know. That's pretty important." And he kissed her soundly. "But you're right. Something's come up. At least I *think* something's come up. Let's sit over here, sweetheart," he said, indicating the leather sofa. "Would you like some coffee?"

"No, thanks. I had coffee hours ago. I'm running late this morning."

"I noticed."

"So…what's come up?"

"Mary Alice was just up here. She's not returning to work after the first of the year. She told me she's getting married and moving away."

Lori digested that. "I wonder…could I possibly have been one-hundred percent wrong about Luke's motives?"

"Lori…sweetheart, I have this feeling…. If she leaves town, we may never solve that theft. All Audit will find is two thousand dollars missing, and I'll look like the world's most incompetent ass."

Lori looked away and chewed her bottom lip.

"And I have a feeling you're getting ready to ask me to do something I'm not going to want to do."

"I'm afraid you're right. If it becomes necessary, will you tell Mary Alice about the phone calls you made?"

Lori gasped. "Oh, Cody…I'd rather die than do that!"

"I know, and I won't ask you to unless it's absolutely necessary. First, I'm going to try something else. I hope I don't end up with a lawsuit on my hands."

He stood, returned to his desk and punched the intercom. "Martha, would you ask Mary Alice to come up here again?"

"Certainly."

Cody released the button and sat back, tapping his mouth with a finger.

Lori's curiosity ran rampant. "What are you doing?"

"Damned if I know. Playing with fire probably." He reached in his desk and pulled out the withdrawal slip that had started it all.

A minute or so passed before Martha announced Mary Alice. The teller entered the office and glanced in Lori's direction. "Hi, Lori. That's a pretty dress."

Lori swallowed hard. "Thank you."

"You wanted to see me, Mr. Hendricks?"

"Yes, Mary Alice, I do. Come here, please. I have a rather odd request to make of you. I hope you don't mind."

"No, sir. Anything."

Cody shoved a piece of paper and a ballpoint toward her. "I want you to write the name Debbie on this paper."

"Debbie?"

"Yes."

"D-e-b-b-i-e?"

Shrugging, Mary Alice bent over the desk and wrote the name. Then she shoved it back toward Cody.

He studied the signatures. They were nothing alike, but wouldn't someone signing a fake signature try to disguise the handwriting? He'd need an expert, and he didn't happen to have one.

Mary Alice stood at the desk, looking at Cody with puzzled eyes. "May...may I ask what this is all about?" Her voice shook, as though she was only now beginning to suspect something was wrong.

"Mary Alice, if I asked you to, would you take a lie detector test?"

Across the room, Lori sucked in her breath and closed her eyes.

"A lie detector test? But how could I have lied about anything? No one's asked me anything. Is…is that standard procedure when someone leaves the bank?"

"Please sit down, Mary Alice. There are some things I'd like to tell you."

She took one of the chairs facing the desk. She sat ramrod straight, eyes focused squarely on Cody.

"Last October," he said, "two thousand dollars was withdrawn from Carolyn Trent's account without her knowledge. The withdrawal slip was signed 'Debbie.' But Debbie Watson initials her transactions."

"Someone stole money from this bank?" Mary Alice asked incredulously. "Gee!" Suddenly her hand flew to her chest. "You think *I* did it?"

"Everyone who handles money has been suspect," Cody said gently.

"I can't believe anyone would think for a minute I would take fifteen cents from this bank!" Mary Alice was very agitated. "I told you—this bank has been a second home to me. Mama and I could never have gotten along without my salary. Why would I do anything to jeopardize that?"

An agitated woman who was near tears was not

something Cody found easy to deal with. Glancing toward Lori, his eyes asked for help.

Lori didn't know which person she felt more sorry for. Standing, she went to put a comforting hand on Mary Alice's shoulder. "If you didn't do anything, Mary Alice, you have nothing to be worried about. Cody...er, Mr. Hendricks is only trying to get to the bottom of a problem. Just answer his questions truthfully, and everything will be fine."

"I *am* answering truthfully. Lori, you don't think I would do something like that, do you?"

"It's...not something I've wanted to believe, I promise you that."

Mary Alice faced Cody squarely. "I don't steal," she said defiantly. "Did you ask everyone to take a lie detector test?"

"No," Cody admitted.

"Then why me?"

Cody looked at Lori, who drew a deep breath. She bent slightly and faced Mary Alice. "I'm afraid you have been suspected mainly because...because of your involvement with Luke Harte."

"Luke?" Mary Alice cried. "What does he have to do with any of this?"

"We don't know," Lori said. "Maybe nothing.

But we have to ask questions. Just be patient with us. You've been with the bank a long time, so you know how serious embezzlement is.''

Embezzlement? Mary Alice was becoming more confused by the minute. It was all so crazy...weird, really. Stolen money...and none of the other tellers was in this office answering questions. She was! And some of those questions were about Luke. Why? Was he in some kind of trouble? Was that why she couldn't find him? Was he maybe not coming back? She'd never been so frightened in her life.

CHAPTER TWELVE

MARY ALICE RUBBED her throbbing temples. This had turned out to be the worst day of her life, absolutely the worst. First, she didn't know where Luke was, and now she had been accused of stealing money. "I don't understand what Luke has to do with this," she repeated.

Lori sat in the other chair and leaned toward the teller, speaking earnestly. "Have you ever given him money?"

"Y-yes, of course, many times. He doesn't make much, you know, and he's been saving like crazy. But Luke and I are engaged. It's no one's business if I give him money."

"More specifically," Cody said, "did you give him two thousand dollars in October?"

"Two thousand?" Mary Alice looked at him as if he were crazy. "Of course not. Where would I get two thousand dollars?" Then awareness struck. Her lips pinched together in a tight line.

"You think I stole two thousand dollars from Mrs. Trent's account and gave it to Luke."

"I don't know, Mary Alice," Cody said. "It's just one of the many possibilities I'm exploring."

"Well, it's not a possibility, not even a remote one. Why would anyone think that, even for a minute?"

"I don't like telling you this," Lori said, "but Luke has a history of getting money from women."

"I don't understand any of this. How do you know that? You don't even know Luke well."

"I'm afraid I made it my business to find out."

"Why, Lori, why? I thought you were my friend."

"I am, and that's why I made the phone calls to places Luke had worked before. I wanted to know what kind of man you'd gotten mixed up with. All down the line the story was the same. Lonely women would give him money, and he would disappear. It didn't happen once or twice, Mary Alice. It happened many times. Luke's nest egg was not acquired through hard work."

Mary Alice's hands twisted nervously. She thought of the five hundred dollars and felt her upset stomach return. But she shook free of her thoughts. She knew Luke, and she was being hor-

ribly disloyal to him by doubting him and his motives for even one second. She owed Lori and Mr.
Hendricks nothing. Soon they wouldn't be part of
her life, but Luke would be everything.

"I've given Luke money, but I certainly didn't
steal it. I saved for years and years to get that five
hundred, and…" She stopped, realizing she was
giving Luke's accusers ammunition.

She was right. Lori put a hand to her head and
groaned. "Oh, Mary Alice, please tell me you
didn't…you didn't give him your savings!"

Mary Alice's chin came up defiantly. "He
needed it to buy the ranch. He had all but five
hundred, and the old rancher wouldn't come down
a penny."

"Did Luke know you had saved five hundred?" Lori asked.

"I…guess so."

"Didn't it strike you as odd that he lacked exactly the amount you had in your savings account?"

"No! Why are you involved in this, Lori? This
is bank business. Why would *you* be the one to
call around and spy on Luke?"

Lori felt her face flush. "I…I heard some
things about Luke that alarmed me. I was worried
about you."

"Well, I just wish everyone would leave me alone."

Cody had been watching the exchange between the women, and something had occurred to him. The missing two thousand dollars seemed of far less importance to Mary Alice than the awful things that were being said about Luke. She appeared to be angry, not scared or worried. It was an interesting observation but one he hadn't yet had time to analyze.

"Mary Alice," Lori was saying, "have you actually seen this ranch Luke is buying?"

"I...no, I..."

"Where is it?"

"It's twenty miles from Fort Worth."

"Where is Luke now?"

"I'm sure he's on his way back from Fort Worth. He went up there over the weekend to wrap up the deal. He's probably already back. There's probably a message for me downstairs."

No, Lori thought, Mary Alice's money was probably on its way to parts unknown. Lori wanted to kick herself. She should have warned Mary Alice the minute she had talked to Luke's former employers. Perhaps the young woman wouldn't have believed her, but she might have planted just enough doubt in her mind to make

her think twice before giving Luke her life savings. "Oh, Mary Alice," she moaned. "I'm
sorry...so sorry."

"Sorry? Sorry for what?" The teller suddenly
jumped to her feet and squared her shoulders,
tossing her long blond hair as she did. Lori
thought what a completely uncharacteristic gesture that was.

"I don't have to stay here and listen to any
more of this!" Mary Alice declared emphatically.
"None of the things you're thinking about Luke
are true. If someone told you they are, they're
lying." She whirled toward Cody, eyes blazing.
"Mr. Hendricks, any time you want me to take a
lie detector test, you just say the word. And in the
meantime...in the meantime, I just might think
about getting myself a lawyer."

Turning on her heel, she went to the door and
angrily flung it open. Then she stopped dead in
her tracks. "Luke!" she cried.

Lori and Cody exchanged startled glances, then
craned their necks. From where she sat, Lori saw
Luke Harte uncurl from one of the chairs in the
outer office.

"Hi, sugar," he drawled with a lazy grin. "One
of the tellers told me you were up here, so I
thought I'd come up and wait for you."

"Where have you been?" she demanded. "I've been worried sick. I couldn't even sleep last night."

"Hey, things took longer than I thought they would."

"You could have called."

Luke walked to her and put a hand on her shoulder. "I didn't say positively when I'd be back. What's the matter with you anyway? Why do you have that funny look on your face?"

Mary Alice's shoulders sagged. She slipped her arms around his waist and hugged him ferociously. "Oh, I'm so glad to see you."

"Good grief, you'd think I'd been gone a month."

Mary Alice took him by the hand. "Come in here, Luke. Just come with me. I want you to hear the terrible things they're saying about you."

"About me? Why would anyone be saying terrible things about me?"

She propelled him back into the office and closed the door. Luke glanced around, a perplexed expression on his face. "I sure would like to know what the hell is going on here," he said.

Mary Alice waved a hand in Lori's direction. "Luke, this is Lori Porter."

"Yes, I know. We've met."

Lori acknowledged the cowboy with a nod and a wan smile.

"And I think you've met Mr. Hendricks, my boss."

Cody got to his feet and shook Luke's outstretched hand. "Have a seat, young man." When Luke was seated, Cody sat down, rubbing the bridge of his nose. Damned if he didn't feel a headache coming on. He had no idea where all this was heading, but he had a feeling it was in no direction that he had previously envisioned.

He was wondering if there was a tactful way to get the confrontation going when Mary Alice saved him the trouble of trying. "They think I stole money from the bank, Luke," she said.

Luke stared at her in disbelief for a second or two, then turned to Cody and chuckled. "Mary Alice? If you knew her as well as I do, you'd know she's the last person in the world who would steal anything, much less money."

"Actually, Luke, almost everybody in the bank was suspect," Cody said.

"Well, everybody else might have done it, but not Mary Alice."

Lori noticed the fond smile Luke bestowed on Mary Alice, and her hopes rose. The smile looked genuine. He was back, wasn't he, *after* Mary Alice had given him her savings. Could Hank finally have come up with a dream that was pure imagination?

"They also thought you had something to do with it," Mary Alice told Luke.

"Me?"

Cody decided he'd better take charge before this thing jumped the track. "Tell me, Luke…did someone give you two thousand dollars in October?"

"How in hell did you find out about that?"

"So someone did."

The cowboy hesitated, his eyes narrowing suspiciously. Then he relaxed and shrugged. "Maybe."

Mary Alice gasped and turned to him, clamping her bottom lip between her teeth, but Luke didn't look in her direction.

The hint of a smile played at the corners of Cody's mouth. *Hank, you're incredible!* "Do you mind telling me who it was?"

"As a matter of fact, I do," Luke said with cool indifference. "The person in question might not like it. It was a personal matter."

Lori studied Mary Alice and realized that all this was news to her. No matter what the outcome of all this proved to be, Mary Alice apparently

was guilty of nothing but poor judgment in choosing a boyfriend. Lori was absolutely positive the
teller had not withdrawn that money, and she
couldn't have been more pleased. For one thing,
it renewed her confidence in her intuition.

"Luke, if you'd cooperate with us," Cody said,
"you might help us quietly clear up an important
matter without having to resort to a full-scale audit."

"Look, what you people have to resort to is
your affair. I'm not going to tell you who gave
me that money, so you're wasting your breath."

"Did you work for it?"

"You could say that. Mostly it was just a gift."

"People are in the habit of giving you gifts in
the form of money, aren't they?"

Luke frowned. "What are you talking about?"

"The woman in Amarillo. The sisters in Kerrville. And there were others. There were always
lonely women around who were willing to give
you large sums of money."

Lori noticed that Luke's unconcern seemed to
slip a bit. Maybe he realized Mary Alice was
hearing things he'd rather she not.

"Seems to me the people in this bank have
damned little to do if investigating my past is so
important to you."

"Why did they give you money, Luke?" Cody continued the grilling, speaking in a soft, measured voice.

"Look, you might think you're dealing with a hayseed, but I'm no dummy. I know I don't have to answer questions like this. I don't work for you. I haven't done anything to you…or to anyone else, for that matter."

"If you haven't done anything, you shouldn't mind answering my questions. What did you do to earn the money the women gave you?"

"Not much really."

"Did you ask them for it?"

"No, never."

"They just offered the money to you?"

"That's about it."

"You never promised them anything in return?"

"Never."

Lori thought Luke was insufferable, but she believed him. She didn't think he was more or less than an unconscionable opportunist. Her glance went back to Mary Alice, who looked thunderstruck.

And what was Cody doing? Treading on dangerous ground, that was what. He had no business asking these questions, and he surely knew that.

"You'll have to forgive me, Luke," Cody said, "but I find that hard to believe."

"I don't give a damn what you believe. You're not the law." He turned to Mary Alice and frowned when he saw the look on her face. Eyes flashing angrily, he turned back to Cody. "Okay, Mr. Banker, I'm going to give you a lesson in life, and then Mary Alice and I are splitting. We don't have to sit here and listen to this crap.

"Look, the world is just full of people nobody pays any attention to. They don't have anybody to talk to. Nobody ever tells 'em they look nice or cook good food. They don't have anybody to mend a step or put a new lock on the door, and I can't help it if most of them are women. A little bit of your time, a few kind words, run a few errands for 'em, trim a hedge, paint a garage door, and they'd give you the moon if they could. It's kinda pitiful really."

"Isn't that totally unscrupulous?" Cody asked.

"Hey, like I said—I didn't ask anyone for a thing. They all knew I was strapped for funds, and I'm not an idiot. I've been a working stiff all my life. My parents gave me zilch, zero. If someone says, 'Please take this money. I'd feel so much better if you did. It would be a small token of appreciation for all you've done for me,' you think I'm gonna turn it down? Get real.''

Mary Alice uttered a little whimper. Luke reached for her hand, but she jerked it away. Jumping to her feet, she glared down at him. ''You've never trimmed a hedge or run any errands for Mama and me. For sure you haven't painted anything for us. You've never so much as changed a faucet washer in our house. Is that why I never see you on Fridays? Are you out buttering up some poor lonely woman?'' Whirling, she ran out of the office, her hand over her eyes.

The look Luke gave Cody was murderous. ''Now see what you've done. I'll have to talk till I'm blue before she's all sweet again.''

''I didn't do a thing,'' Cody said. ''Did you really buy a ranch over the weekend?''

''Man, you've got more nerve than anybody I've ever met, but since you're so damned interested in my personal life, yes, I did.'' His eyes radiated insolence as he reached into his shirt pocket and withdrew some folded papers. Shoving them toward Cody, he said, ''Here's the deed to the place. Look it over good.''

Cody barely glanced at the document before handing it back to Luke. ''And you and Mary Alice are really getting married?''

Luke rolled his eyes. "How would you like it if I asked you about *your* love life, assuming you have one?"

"Are you?"

"Yeah…or we were. If you haven't queered the deal, we still will."

"Luke, may I ask you a question?" Lori's voice cut through the tense atmosphere in the room.

Luke glared at her. "Might as well. Can't be any worse than the ones the banker's asking."

"Given your reputation as…well, as sort of a drifter who doesn't settle down…why Mary Alice?"

"What do you mean 'why'? I fell in love, that's why! I sure as hell didn't plan on it. Junk happens."

Lori took a deep breath. *He fell in love. It was as simple as that. Why didn't I ever once consider the possibility?*

"Luke, I'd like to ask you one more question," Cody said.

"Oh, good God! You never get tired, do you? Okay, what's the question?"

"The person who gave you the two thousand dollars—is he or she associated with this bank?"

Luke shook his head. "No way am I going to answer that."

"Were you aware that the money had been stolen from this bank?"

A moment of silence passed. Then to Cody's and Lori's complete astonishment, Luke burst out laughing. "Stolen? Boy, Mr. Banker, now I know you're way off base. Shoot, Mrs. Merriwether doesn't have to steal money. She's loaded with the stuff."

CHAPTER THIRTEEN

SHOCKED SILENCE filled the room. Lori and Cody looked at each other, disbelieving. It was Cody who finally spoke. "Helen Merriwether?"

"Well, I didn't really mean to tell you that. You caught me off guard with that garbage about the money being stolen."

"Why would Helen give you money?"

Luke got to his feet, his arrogance restored. "Ask the lady herself that, why don't you? Now, thanks to you, I've got to go do some fence-mending." He sauntered out of the office, closing the door behind him with more force than necessary.

"Charming young man," Cody said.

"He's insufferable. Poor Mary Alice. I hope in time she'll see it was worth five hundred dollars to be rid of him."

"Do you suppose she really will get rid of him?"

Lori smiled ruefully. "Maybe not. She was

deeply in love, and apparently he's a smooth talker. She just might end up with him after all. If she does stay with him, I hope she gives him a good scare first.''

''I guess you're feeling awfully good about this.''

''I'm glad Mary Alice isn't the thief, yes.''

''Helen Merriwether, of all people!'' Cody shook his head.

''Cody, all we know is that Helen gave Luke two thousand dollars. That doesn't prove it was stolen. It's always seemed to me that Helen is pretty well-off financially. So it looks like you're back to square one, without a clue to stand on.''

''I'm not so sure. I have a hunch.''

Lori made a scoffing sound. ''You also had a hunch about Mary Alice.''

He nodded solemnly. ''I know, but I'd make a poor detective. I forgot the modus operandi. Luke's benefactors were always older, lonely women with money. Mary Alice never fit. I'm sorry to say I had her guilty by association. But Helen fits…to a T.'' He punched the intercom. ''Martha, send Helen Merriwether up here, please.''

Lori's eyes widened. ''Cody! You can't do this! You know nothing, nothing.''

"Yes, I do."

"How can you?"

"Hank."

"Oh, Lord." Lori put a hand to her temple. "I'm sure this isn't a procedure you learned in Banking 101."

"I believe in UFOs, remember. I believe a hundred-year-old man can 'see' oil underground. I don't think like your average banker, something my father has mentioned to me about a hundred times."

"You're not...you can't just come right out and accuse Helen of stealing."

"I know that. Please...give me credit for having a little sense."

"I don't feel good about this."

"Trust me."

The intercom's buzzer sounded. "Yes, Martha."

"Helen is here, Mr. Hendricks."

"Send her in."

Helen entered the office, looking very chic in a gray and burgundy dress that perfectly complemented her silver hair. She was the picture of everyone's favorite grandmother, Lori thought. She recalled Helen's past accomplishments—tireless United Way volunteer, past president of Business and Professional Women, a stalwart at First Baptist Church.

But also a lonely widow with some money.

"You want to see me, Mr. Hendricks?" she asked.

"Yes, Helen. Please have a seat."

As Helen took a chair, she turned to Lori. "Hello, Lori. You look awfully pretty this morning."

"Thank you, Helen," Lori replied, her stomach sinking like a brick in water.

Helen then gave Cody her full attention. He cleared his throat and began. "Helen, do you recall a day some weeks back when there was a problem with an account Carolyn Trent came in to close out?"

Helen shifted in her chair. "Y-yes, sir, I do."

"We never have found that money."

"Really? I just assumed when you told me to transfer the entire amount that…everything was all right."

"Well, that was a judgment call of mine that might not have been exactly wise. Tell me, you know all the tellers. You work closely with them, and I assume some of them even confide in you. Do you know anyone who might be having a problem of some sort?"

"Problem? I...don't think so."

"Marital, financial, anything of that nature?"

"No, not that I know of."

"I see." Cody pretended to be deep in thought for a second or two; then he sighed. "Well, I had hoped I wouldn't have to do this, but it can't be helped."

"Do what, sir?" Helen asked.

"Call everyone up from the floor, one by one, and ask them to take a lie detector test."

"How embarrassing!"

"True, and I'm well aware that they all have the right to refuse. However, a refusal would immediately make that person a prime suspect. I dislike doing it, but I don't know what else to do. We're due for an internal audit after the first of the year. If I don't find that money before then, I'll doubtless lose my job."

"Oh, Mr. Hendricks, I would hate that. It's been wonderful working for you, and morale has been so high here since you came on board."

Cody gave her his warmest smile. "Thank you, Helen. Well, I guess that will be all. I'd appreciate it if you didn't mention this to anyone. Things are apt to get difficult in the next few days."

Helen swallowed hard, glanced at Lori, then down at her hands. When her eyes came back up, she asked, "What will happen to whoever took the money?"

"Nothing, if restitution is made."

"I see." Helen hesitated a minute, then said, "You can save yourself a lot of trouble, Mr. Hendricks. There's no need to embarrass the others. I took the money from Carolyn's account."

Cody and Lori exchanged quick glances before he faced Helen. "You?"

"Yes. I was going to pay the money back at the end of this month. You see, that's when I get my yearly allowance from Henry's trust."

"How could you pay it back? There's no account to put it back in."

"I know. I must say I was awfully upset when Carolyn came in to close that account. Then when you sent word down to me to pay her the full amount that her passbook showed, I worried about it quite a bit for a few days. For weeks afterward, every morning when I came to work I half expected the place to be crawling with bank examiners. But as time passed, and nothing happened, I thought...well, when I got my allowance I'd just put two thousand dollars in an envelope and address it to you. If the money was returned, I figured that would be the end of it. Two thousand dollars wasn't enough for anyone to make a big fuss over.''

"And you signed Debbie Watson's name to the withdrawal slip?''

Helen nodded humbly.

"Do you realize you implicated a co-worker? Didn't that bother you?''

"Not really. I was sure nothing would happen to Debbie because she hadn't done anything.'' Helen's eyes were as guileless as a child's. "I mean, you'd have to prove she took the money, and since she hadn't, you couldn't, could you?''

Cody uttered a disbelieving laugh and rubbed his eyes tiredly. "All right, Helen. Let me ask you something else. Did you take the money to give to Luke Harte?''

Helen looked startled. "How do you know that?''

"So you did.''

"Yes.''

"Why?''

"He needed it, and he'd been so good to me. My goodness, if you knew all the things he's done to my house and yard, to say nothing of all the errands he's run. I've tried and tried to hire a handyman, but no one seems to want to do that kind of work anymore. Luke gave up all his Friday evenings to help me out, and he never would let me pay him for anything. He even brought me a bottle of cologne once. I hadn't had a present since long before Henry died. When Luke told me he had been saving for years and still needed two thousand dollars...well, I wanted to do something for him. It was his birthday, and I thought it would be the loveliest surprise.''

''So you just helped yourself to Carolyn's money?''

''Y-yes. I really hated doing that, but Carolyn never touched it, and I planned on having it back in the account before the end of the year. It was just my luck that she decided to close it when she did.''

Cody looked at Lori as if to say, *Do you believe any of this?* Then he returned his attention to Helen. ''I guess my next question is obvious. Why did you feel you had to steal, Helen? I know the size of your trust.''

Helen's lips compressed tightly. ''I know it's a tidy fortune, but unfortunately, Henry always thought I was too extravagant. He tied one hand behind my back when he made his will. He made sure I only get a certain amount every year, and it's an irrevocable trust. There's no way I can get more than fifty thousand every December. I've

just never been able to make it last all year. By
October I'm always living from paycheck to paycheck. I'm really going to try to be more frugal
this coming year. It's going to be my New Year's
resolution.''

"Tell me something," Cody said. "Did Luke
tell you his mother needed an operation?''

Helen looked surprised. "No. I didn't know his
mother needed an operation. He said he wanted
to buy a ranch and get married.''

Lori stood up and walked to the window,
slowly shaking her head.

Behind her, Cody was speaking. "Helen, why
the devil didn't you just borrow the money? You
have excellent credit here.''

"But then I'd have to pay interest," Helen said,
as if that was the most logical explanation in the
world. "Henry never borrowed money. He hated
paying interest, and I guess some of that rubbed
off on me.''

Cody was at a loss for words.

"Is...is anyone downstairs going to know
about this?'' Helen asked fearfully.

"It won't go out of this room," Cody promised.

"Am I going to lose my job, Mr. Hendricks?''

"Of course you're going to lose your job!''

The woman sighed. "Oh, that's such a shame. I don't know what I'll do with my time if I don't work. If I pay the money back and promise never to do such a thing again...?"

Cody simply stared at her a minute, unable to believe his ears. He knew Helen wasn't stupid. Did she really regard this as little more than a prank? "If the big shots in Houston ever learned I'd uncovered an embezzler and kept her on the payroll, I'd lose *my* job."

"Who would tell them?"

Cody threw up his hands. "That'll be all for now, Helen. I'm...I'm going to have to think this thing through."

"Yes, sir. May I go back to my desk?"

"Yes, yes," he said impatiently.

"Thank you." Helen looked in Lori's direction. "Lori, you won't tell Carolyn...."

Lori turned from the window. "Of course not."

"Thank you so much." Helen turned to Cody. "Mr. Hendricks, I have a suggestion. Why don't you just take the two thousand out of my trust, and all this will be over and done with?" With that, she pivoted and left the office.

At her teller's station, Mary Alice watched Helen descend the stairs and return to her desk. She felt so miserable she wanted to die. It was on the tip of her tongue to tell Gina she really was sick and needed to go home. She *was* sick—heartsick.

She finished cashing a customer's check and did her best to give him a cheerful smile. When he walked away from the window, Luke stepped up. Mary Alice glared at him.

"I told you to go away," she whispered quietly.

"I'm not leaving until you talk to me."

"There's nothing to say."

"Please, Mary Alice..."

"Keep your voice down."

"I'm going to start yelling to high heaven if you don't come out here and talk to me."

Mary Alice glanced at Gina, who was giving her a peculiar look. The entire day had been disastrous, and she didn't want to cap it by being responsible for a public disturbance. She placed the sign in the window, and with a toss of her head instructed Luke to follow her to the employee lounge in the basement. Thankfully, it was empty.

Once she'd closed the door, she turned to him with stormy eyes. "There's nothing you can say to me that will change my mind," she snapped. "You can't have a conscience to do what you did."

"Ah, for cryin' out loud, I accepted some gifts, that's all. *Gifts!* Hasn't anyone ever given you anything?"

"Very little." Mary Alice was determined not to break down, not to let him see how heartbroken she was. She just wanted to stay mad. "They were more than gifts, Luke, and you know it. You used people shamefully."

"I never hurt anybody. All those people who gave me money really wanted to."

"They thought your mother needed an operation. What you did was...was unethical."

"Mary Alice...sugar..." He put a hand on her shoulder and rubbed gently. Her chin came up, but some of the fire went out of her eyes. "The ranch, remember? It's ours now. Your mama won't have to work anymore. It's gonna be so nice. Tell you what—beginning tomorrow, I'll start painting and fixing up your house. If I hurry and give it my all, we can still leave after New Year's. Then we'll put the house on the market and use the money we get to fix up the ranch house. You want a mauve bedroom, you'll get it. Maybe there'll be enough to buy a good used truck. It's gonna be heaven, sugar." He paused to monitor her reaction. She remained unmoved. "And, okay, if you want a real wedding, you can have it. Nothing big and fancy, you understand, but we can get married in a church, and you can invite your friends.''

Something fluttered inside Mary Alice just then, and she hated herself for it. But the things he had just said—they were all she'd ever wanted. She thought of what life would be like if she stuck to her guns and Luke went to Fort Worth alone. Awful, simply awful. Barren and lonely again. Maybe the things she felt for him didn't make sense, but she couldn't help feeling them. So he wasn't a saint. Neither was she.

She lowered her eyes, then raised her head and projected a confidence she didn't feel. ''No, I'll tell you what we're going to do when we sell the house. We're going to pay back all those people who gave you money, every last cent, before we spend a penny on ourselves.''

Luke looked incredulous. ''Aw, sugar, those people don't want their money back.''

''I mean it, Luke. Every last cent. Then when we get to the ranch, I'm going to get a job at a bank somewhere until we're operating in the black. And *I'm* going to keep the books. I won't rest until all those people get their money back. That's the way it's going to be…or I won't go with you.''

Seconds of silence ticked by. On one hand, Mary Alice was scared to death she was throwing away everything she'd ever wanted. On the other, she was proud of herself for having the courage to say those things. She had surprised herself, and Luke looked positively stunned. He probably hadn't dreamed she had it in her. She hadn't, either.

Finally a lazy smile crossed his face, and he shrugged nonchalantly. "Well...if you say so, I guess that's the way it'll have to be." Bending his head, he kissed her.

When he broke the kiss, Mary Alice's mouth curved into a smile of self-satisfaction. *Funny how easy it was to get my way,* she thought. *All I had to do was stand up for myself. I hope I remember that next week, next month, next year.*

UPSTAIRS, Lori had returned to one of the chairs facing Cody's desk. Over and over, he was muttering, "I don't believe it. I don't believe it."

"Are you going to fire Helen?" Lori asked.

"*Of course* I'm going to fire her. Come on, Lori, be sensible."

"You know she'll never do anything like that again. Caro told me Helen's been with this bank practically from the day it opened its doors."

"For Pete's sake, I can't keep an embezzler on the payroll!"

"She didn't take the money for her personal gain. It was Luke...and whatever he has that appeals to women. Personally, it escapes me. To me, he comes across as nothing but an arrogant ass."

"I still say I'd like to tail him for a couple of days."

"About Helen?"

Cody sighed and stared vacantly into space for a few seconds. "Well...I'll have a long talk with her. Maybe I can put her in a position where she doesn't handle money."

"Thanks."

"You don't know how relieved I am it's over. No more wondering if I'm overlooking something. No more suspecting my employees."

"No more worrying about calling Audit."

"That, too."

Lori nodded and stood. "Well, I guess I'll get back to work."

"Back to the ranch?"

"That's where I work."

"Lori, you can't go." Cody stood and rounded the desk, coming to her and putting his arms loosely around her waist. "Let's blow this joint."

"You're going to leave work on a Monday morning?"

"I just solved a case of embezzlement. That's enough work for one day."

"Where would we go?"

"Home."

"Your house?"

"That's the general idea."

Her eyes dipped, and she fingered his lapel, prompting a frown to furrow his brow. "Is something wrong, Lori?"

"No, nothing's really *wrong*."

"I think there is. I sense something. Having second thoughts, reservations?" When she didn't answer, he asked, "Is it my reputation as a ladies' man, which by the way is a lot of garbage?"

"Oh...not really."

"Is it my family?"

"I...don't think so."

"Then what?"

Lori took a deep breath. "I did a lot of thinking when I went home yesterday."

"I'll swear I'm not letting you out of my sight again. Every time I do, you start thinking. So...what did you think about?"

"You know, things have been moving awfully fast with us."

"Funny. I was trying to come up with a way to speed them up."

"After just a couple of weeks with you, I've found myself thinking I'm in love. Worse, I find myself *wanting* to be in love with you. But realistically, I know I can't be, not yet."

Absolute honesty was the most refreshing thing in the world, Cody thought, possibly because one encountered it so seldom. Lori looked so earnest, so deadly serious, so gorgeous, and to hear her talk about being in love with him made his heart seem to swell to ten times its normal size. "Junk happens."

He pulled her close and kissed her. The kiss was lingering and thorough, the kind that made Lori feel weak, helpless and wonderful all at the same time. When he lifted his mouth from hers, he kissed her eyelids, her forehead, her earlobe. "I think what you really want is a courtship," he said huskily.

Lori pressed her cheek against his chest and slipped her arms around his waist. "Could that be arranged?"

"I think so. I might be a little rusty in that department, but be patient, and I'll get into the swing of it." Smiling, Cody released her and took her by the hand, leading her to the door. "Come on," he said. "One ardent courtship coming up."

EPILOGUE

LORI WAS FULL of a wondrous contentment as she dressed for the gala evening. Cody was the most accomplished lover in the world. She was the object of the most passionate, single-minded court-ship imaginable. Perhaps it was still too soon to know if they would walk blissfully through life hand and hand, but she was thinking along those lines. It felt so right and good, and if it was meant to be, it would be. In the meantime, she intended enjoying every second with him. The past five years had been lonely and lacking in vitality, and the past dozen must have been worse for him. Now they had found each other, and tomorrow held such promise. But Lori didn't dwell on to-morrow much, because today was so wonderful.

The phone on her desk rang. Giving her appearance one last look in the mirror, she went to answer it.

"Lori Porter."

"Lori, darling."

"Grandma?"

"I'm not interrupting anything, am I?"

"No, I just finished dressing. Cody and I are going to Hank's birthday party."

"Whose birthday party?"

"Hank's. Remember J.T. McKinney's grandfather?"

Lori heard Anna sniff. "Oh, yes. The crotchety old man." Anna had met Hank once. It had not been an auspicious encounter.

"He's one hundred today."

"You don't say. I guess it's true that some people are too ornery to die. Listen, darling, I'm making my plans for Christmas. You will be here Christmas Eve, won't you?"

"Of course. In fact, I'm bringing Cody with me."

There was a gasp of delight. "Lori, how wonderful!"

"Grandma, we're merely spending Christmas Eve together. Please don't do or say anything embarrassing. Don't book the church yet."

"Speaking of church, I know you don't go anymore, but I was wondering if you would attend midnight Mass with me this year."

"I would love to, Grandma."

"Really?"

"Of course, really."

There was a long pause, then Anna said, "Then I want you to do a favor for me."

"Anything."

"When we get to the church, I want you to go inside a few minutes before I do."

A most peculiar request, Lori thought. "Well, okay, but...why?"

"So if the roof falls in, I won't get hurt."

Lori chortled. "You got it, Grandma. A full two minutes. Now, I've got to run. Cody will be here any minute."

"Goodbye, darling. Have a wonderful time. And tell that horrible old man I said happy birthday."

A STEADY STREAM of cars and trucks poured through the Double C's front gate and up the road to the ranch house. Lori had never seen such a crowd for a private party. She couldn't honestly say the cantankerous Hank was well loved by the local citizens, but the McKinneys were. And a one-hundredth birthday was a milestone everyone wanted to celebrate.

Inside the house, Lori and Cody found a crush of guests. A lavish buffet had been set up in the dining room, and Virginia and Lettie Mae were scurrying about with their usual efficiency. J.T. and Cynthia stood near the front door to greet the guests, and the birthday celebrant was seated in a chair near the roaring hearth, holding court as he was surrounded by well-wishers. It was impossible to get close to Hank right away, so Lori and Cody mingled with the guests and waited for their chance.

It came later, when the crowd had thinned out considerably. "Hello, Hank," Lori said, coming to stand in front of him. "Is this the proudest day of your life?"

"Hell, no! Not by a country mile." The old man shifted his gaze to Cody. "Howdy, young feller."

"Good evening, Hank. Happy birthday."

"Still can't believe I've had so goddamn many of them. Know somethin', I've been thinkin' about you. Wondered if I was able to help you with your little problem."

"You certainly did. I can't thank you enough."

"Think nothin' of it." Hank looked at Lori. "Seems to me you two's spendin' an awful lot of time together. You thinkin' about gettin' hitched or somethin'?"

Lori laughed, but Cody was serious. "Yes, we are."

Hank cackled and winked at Lori. "This one ain't half bad for a banker."

"I agree."

Hank's attention returned to Cody. "Had time to think about that oil?"

Cody had been converted into a true believer, and he actually had done some thinking about the oil Hank had seen. But he knew there was no chance the old man could get a loan. "I've been very busy these past few weeks," he said, briefly giving Lori a pointed glance, "but I have done some thinking. Why don't you forget about a loan and go after some investors? People in the upper brackets who can use the tax write-offs if the well's dry."

"It ain't gonna come up no duster," Hank said. "I can promise you that. You can't go wrong dealin' with me in the oil bi'ness, 'cause I'm one lucky feller, and luck's what you need more of than smarts."

"So I've heard," Cody said.

"Reminds me of ol' Tiny Sparburger. Never did tell you about Tiny, did I?"

"No, Hank, I don't think you did."

"Tiny had an ol' hardscrabble ranch out in West Texas, must'a been in about '29 or '30, somethin' like that, and a wildcatter found a drop or two of oil on the place. It wasn't a big well or anythin' close, but it put some money in Tiny's pocket for the first time in his life. So he got the notion to do a little prospectin' on his own.'' Again Hank cackled. ''Now he didn't know beans from wild honey about drillin' for oil, but that didn't stop him. He bought an old wooden rig from a prospector who'd gone belly-up and started diggin' holes. Know what? Ever' well ol' Tiny dug came up squirtin' clean over the derrick. Know why?''

''He was lucky?'' Lori ventured.

Hank looked at her with new admiration. ''The luckiest son of a bitch I ever heard of. And that reminds me of Elmer Scruggins. Never did tell you about Elmer, did I?''

''No, I don't think so,'' Cody said with a smile.

''Elmer had a little bitty farm near Kilgore, and in about '32, I guess it was, he…''

Lori found a chair, sat down and motioned for Cody to do the same. She knew from experience they were going to be there a while.

Welcome back to the drama and mystery that is the Fortune Dynasty

Membership of the glamorous Fortune family has its privileges...and its price! But even the wealthy Fortunes can't buy love—that comes naturally!

Fortune's Heirs is a 16 book continuity with two new books every month. Don't miss book one at the special price of £1.50

FH/RTL/1aa

Fortune's Heirs

The Romance
Collection

SENSATION

Prince Joe
Suzanne Brockmann

DESIRE

The Five-Minute Bride
Leanne Banks

SPECIAL EDITION

Molly Darling
Laurie Paige

Only £3.99

On sale 23rd December 2000

0101/SH/SH6

The romance you'd want

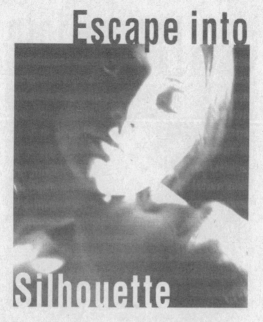

Escape into

Silhouette

DESIRE®

Intense, sensual love stories.

Desire™ are short, fast and sexy romances featuring alpha males and beautiful women. They can be intense and they can be fun, but they always feature a happy ending.

GEN/22/RTL

The romance you'd want

Escape into

Silhouette
SPECIAL EDITION ®

*Vivid, satisfying romances, full of family,
life and love*

Special Editions are romances between attractive
men and women. Family is central to the plot. The
novels are warm upbeat dramas grounded in reality
with a guaranteed happy ending.

GEN/23/RTL